ZEKE'S HERITAGE

A JESSIE WEAVER WESTERN ADVENTURE

BOOK 4

WILLIAM TRESLER

CHAPTER I

CHANGES

Zeke Nugent's heart beat a wild tattoo in rhythm with the rapid thrumming of Hoedown's hooves on the sandy valley floor. He dared not glance back for fear of unsettling his horse and giving the rider behind him even that slight bit of an advantage. With each thrust of his powerful hindquarters, Hoedown increased the distance between himself and the horse behind him.

Zeke knew the horse needed little urging. Hoedown was as anxious as he was to lose the horse and rider behind them in their dust, but still he swung his left hand back and forth, whooping and hawing with the sheer exhilaration of the chase. As fast as the other rider's horse was, Zeke knew he and Hoedown were safe. They always were. There wasn't a horse in the entire Colorado Territory that could catch Hoedown.

At last the horse crossed the wide line in the soil, dug just deep enough to be seen but not deep enough to trip up a horse. Zeke flung his hat in the air with an extra loud whoop and slapped his mount's sweat-streaked neck exuberantly. "Yee-haw! We done it again, Hoedown, you old firecracker, you!" he yelled.

Hoedown tossed his head and slowed his gallop, but he was still full of oats. The powerful Nez Percé horse would go for another quarter mile, probably more, if Zeke didn't pull him in. But the young man, feeling the mettle of his twenty-one years and some magical flow of energy between himself and the horse he rode, left Hoedown to let off a little more steam.

They liked to do that, the pair of them. It had become almost a habit to do a little victory loop at the end of a quarter-mile racetrack. And the losers behind them usually reined in their mounts to a rock-scattering halt and turned tail for home in abject defeat.

Not this time.

Hoedown slowed, treading hot bricks. Zeke looked around, trying to locate his hat. A thunder of hooves filled his ears. Before Zeke knew what was happening, the man he'd been racing rode his horse right up against Hoedown, making the horse shy and catching Zeke off balance.

A rough hand grabbed his upper arm, pulling him from the saddle and down to the ground. In that instant, Zeke felt his instincts kick in. It had been eight long years since he'd needed his wits as badly as that moment, but it was like time hadn't passed.

He landed on his feet, wrenching his arm free, both fists already clenched. The man on the other horse had leaped from the saddle, too, and Zeke got the man in his sights, just in time to duck a brutal, well-knuckled fist aimed at his head. The man grunted from the effort and teetered off balance for a split second as his swing failed to connect.

Zeke took the opportunity and came up, planting a snapping left jab just below the man's ribs. The man doubled over, gasping for breath, and Zeke swung in a wicked right uppercut at the man's face. His knuckles hit a cheekbone, splitting the skin and drawing first blood.

"You thievin' chiseler! I won't stand for no Indian and his paint pony cheatin' me out of my winnings!" The man spat as he recoiled to regain his composure and his breath. Eyes full of hatred flashed beneath bushy, knotted brows.

"Now see here, mister," Zeke said, his fists still at the ready. "I won that race fair and square, an' you know it."

"Liar!" the man spat into the dirt at Zeke's feet. "All your kind is liars and thieves and cheats!"

"You might want t' watch your tongue, mister," a low female voice interrupted. Zeke didn't need to turn around to know it was Jessie, the whiskey-drinking, foul-mouthed, rifle-shooting, bronc-gentling gem of a woman who, for the last eight years of Zeke's life, had been mother and friend and sister and coach all rolled into one.

"Yeah," a deep male voice agreed. That would be Tanner, Jessie's husband. "What *kind* exactly were you talking about?"

The man looked incredulous. "Why, any fool with eyes in his head can see this kid's a half-breed Indian. You can take the Indian out of the wild, but you can't take the wild out of the Indian. Nor the cheatin' and thievin'. Why, I'll wager he even stole that dang horse."

"We don't hold with talk like that around here, mister." That was Harold Granger, one of the other homesteaders in Fountain. "If you've got proof of anything, we'll take you straight to the sheriff in Colorado City. Otherwise, you'd be wise to keep your mouth shut if you're figurin' on keepin' all your teeth."

Zeke dared not look around, not trusting the fellow in front of him, but he could sense a crowd was gathering around the two horsemen at the finish line. A strange sense of discomfort began to swirl in his stomach.

Nobody had ever said so, but Zeke had looked into the small oval mirror on his wall many days and wondered why he looked different. Why he felt different. His skin was darker than most of the young men in Fountain. His eyes almost black and almond-shaped, sloping down at the ends. All that redeemed him was his dark brown, curly hair. But even his slightly hooked nose and narrow forehead spoke of a lineage he had long suspected. A suspicion he had never breathed a word of to a single soul.

Now he turned to see the young women standing in the group, the young women who had once only looked on him with hopeful blushes and giggles behind their hands. Now they stood staring at him, as if seeing for the first time the evidence of his own hidden suspicions laid bare by the words of a stranger. In that instant, he knew they saw him differently, although he himself had not changed one jot.

"So that's how it is, eh?" the defeated rider said, grasping his horse's reins and swinging back up into the saddle. "You got yourself a good deal here, boy. Better hang onto it while it lasts."

Zeke started toward the man. What he was going to do to him, he didn't know. All he knew was he had been overtaken by a sudden, consuming, burning rage.

"Don't let him bait you, son," Tanner's voice rang out loud and clear like the sun through the mists of the morning.

The man looked down at Zeke and smiled. It was not a friendly smile. "This ain't the last you'll be seeing of me, half-breed." He put heels to his horse and split the crowd in two as he barged forward.

In an instant, Jessie was at Zeke's side, yelling at the back of the retreating horseman. "You better get ready to face three guns if you ever show your face here again, mister! We'll stand by our boy. You see if we don't!"

Zeke put his hand on her arm. It felt wrong to have a woman defending him. Even if she was the toughest little

Cattle Kate he'd ever known. Even if she had taken him in and treated him like her own son. Even if he knew her heart was made of pure gold.

"Come on, son. Let's go home," Tanner said, appearing at his other side and looping one arm across his shoulders.

Home. He'd called it that for eight years. The first proper home he'd ever known. And yet, in an instant he felt as if everything he'd built in those eight years was a lie, a pretense. All because of some loose-tongued comments from a passerby.

Or had those words simply given life to something that everyone had been pushing to the backs of their minds? Including Zeke himself?

THAT EVENING, he stared at himself in the mirror again. Dipping his comb in the washbasin in front of him, he pulled it through his hair, darkening the strands to nearly black and straightening out the wavy curls. There was no doubt about it. He looked Indian, all right. With the White man's clothes gone and just his reddish brown skin and eyes filled with an intensity that sometimes surprised even himself, there was no more distraction from the glaring facts.

"You about ready to go, Zeke?" Jessie's voice cut through his somber contemplation.

"Yeah, about."

He quickly dressed into his best jeans, a blue and white checked shirt and a fringed, tan rawhide jacket, given to him by Tanner. It was identical to his adoptive father's own jacket, but somehow Tanner didn't look as Indian in it as Zeke felt.

He didn't want to go to the dance anymore. He knew instinctively that barn dances at the Brinzers' place would never be the same. And he was right.

Standing next to Tanner, sipping on a fragrant punch, he looked around the barn. None of the girls batted their eyes at him or cast hopeful glances or inviting smiles in his direction. Instead, they whispered behind their hands and tried to look as if they hadn't noticed him.

Their fathers, who might have nodded and waved in the past when they caught him looking at their daughters, now scowled slightly and subtly placed themselves between their daughters and Zeke's line of sight.

Zeke felt sick to his stomach. The signs were so subtle and so obvious. Who he was didn't seem to matter anymore. What he looked like had suddenly blinded his own community to everything they had always known him to be.

"What's ailing you, son?" Jessie's voice made him jump. "Usually by this time, you've danced with half the young ladies in the room already." She was smiling, a proud, teasing, motherly smile. She chucked her chin at the gaggle of dancers that were just leaving the dance floor at the end of the last dance.

Zeke shrugged, unable to look her in the eye. "I don't know. Guess I'm out of sorts after that fight."

"Then a dance is just what you need to perk you up," Jessie said, squeezing his arm. "How about you go ask Lucy Granger for the next one? The pair of ya always have a fine time of dancing together."

It was true. Lucy was a little firecracker. She always seemed to match his energy and sometimes even challenge it. He always felt good after a dance with Lucy. Maybe Jessie was right. He took a deep breath, squared his shoulders, and sauntered over to where Lucy stood, talking with some of the other girls. "Howdy, Lu," he said, removing his hat and holding out his hand. "You up for a dance?"

Lucy looked up. Her deep blue eyes seemed almost wary, searching. As if they suddenly didn't recognize him and were checking for signs of a threat or some kind of assurance. It felt like a punch to his gut. Those eyes had always sparkled before, those cheeks had always flushed, when he'd asked her to take a spin with him on the dance floor. Now they regarded him almost with suspicion.

Then she smiled. "You know I always love dancing with you, Zeke," she said, accepting his hand. As she did, she glanced to her left.

Zeke followed the direction of her eyes and looked into Harold Granger's face. Harold looked slightly perplexed, as if there were a battle going on inside him. As if he were fighting to keep himself from wrenching his daughter's hand from Zeke's grasp.

Zeke gave the man an acknowledging nod, pushing his thoughts aside. This was the man who'd stood up for him when the stranger called him a thief. And anyhow, why would he have any qualms with his daughter dancing with a man she'd danced with countless times before?

Zeke put it down to his own fears and self-doubt. Goodness knew, he'd struggled with those same things all his life, even while living in the glow of Jessie and Tanner's patient acceptance and wise guidance and counsel. He was seeing things is all. Folks all had things on their minds. Perhaps it was just the fight, like he'd told Jessie.

But the dance wasn't what he was used to either. The sparkle missing from Lucy's eyes was also missing from their dance. Her movements were hesitant and uncertain, her steps felt wooden and forced. Zeke could have sworn she was holding herself back, trying not to get too close or laugh too much.

With his mood darkening, Zeke left the dance floor when the dance was over and headed for the punch bowl. He downed two cups right after each other. The little whiskey in the drink made his head zing for a moment. He looked around, feeling a pit of emptiness sinking into his stomach. Everyone around him, except for Jessie and Tanner, had become strangers, without warning.

What he had always believed to be true felt like a horrible trick played on an innocent child. He didn't really belong here. He wasn't really one of them and he wondered if he ever had been. If that was so, he wasn't Zeke Nugent. He wasn't Zeke Freeman, either, the name he'd given himself. He wasn't Stands And Stares either, the name the Nez Percé tribe had given him as a little boy.

But then, if he wasn't all of those, who was he?

Zeke set down his punch cup, shook the dizzying tendrils of alcohol from his mind, and marched out of the barn. He was almost done saddling up Hoedown when he felt Jessie's hand on his arm.

"Zeke, what's eatin' ya?"

He couldn't see her face in the shadows of night beyond the bright gas lamps of the barn dance, but he knew her question was born of genuine care. "My head hurts," he muttered. It wasn't a lie. All the thoughts tumbling around in his mind were making it hurt. His heart was aching, too, with an ache he was vaguely familiar with. An old ache he'd thought he'd never feel again. But he didn't tell her that.

"All right, you go sleep it off," she said.

It did not fool Zeke. Jessie could read him like a book. She would probably pepper him with questions later. Or somehow wheedle it out of him. It was a bit of a private game they played. Jessie knew just how to get at a body's deepest thoughts without making you feel like they had barged in.

He followed her advice, as he usually did, and tried to sleep when he got back to the cabin. But sleep proved as evasive as the glances of the young homesteader girls at the barn dance.

He lay tossing and turning, the events of the day thrashing about in his head.

At last he drifted off into a restless slumber, busy with dreams.

He was on a horse. It wasn't Hoedown. It was a mean-eyed, Roman-nosed black stallion. Arrows were flying about his head. Bullets whizzed by. Screams and roars of dying and angry men filled his ears. The smell of blood and sweat and dust was thick in his nostrils. A screaming White man, with silver white hair, came at him, spear raised, eyes filled with bloodlust.

Zeke pulled out a pistol he didn't even know he was wearing and shot at his attacker. He heard a cry to his right. Someone was standing there, someone he didn't know, calling his name and asking him for help. The man was dressed in dog soldier garb, his dog rope pinned to the ground. All at once, the man's head and legs turned to those of a dog.

All Zeke knew was that the man was his comrade. He rushed to his side, fighting off a group of men who looked similar to the dog soldier, and yet different. Their skins were white, but their dress was like that of the Pawnee who Zeke had seen scouting for the US Army. Together, he and his dog friend felled the attackers until blood flowed like a red river around their feet.

In the heat of the battle, Zeke looked down and realized his body was not his own. Instead of a man's legs and torso, he saw the hairy legs and paws of a bear. The hatchet he wielded was clenched in the grasp of a bear's paw with long, curving claws.

Zeke cried out, dropping the hatchet and staggering backward. His hands, or paws, flew to his face. Instead of human features, he felt the long, wet-nosed snout of a bear. He roared in fear and confusion and then woke, sweating in his bed.

For a few moments, he stared into the darkness, listening to the pounding of his pulse in his ears as his heart gradually slowed back to a normal rate. Then, remembering what he had just dreamed, he looked down at his arms and belly. There was no dark brown fur or claws. He was still a man.

Zeke got up and went to the window, flinging it wide. Outside, somewhere, a wolf howled. The cry seemed to call to something inside of him. He gripped the windowsill, feeling like a caged animal. Something he had no power over was catching up to him. Something he had ignored for as long as he could remember. That dream. He knew he'd had it before. Many times.

One day he was going to find out what it meant. One day. Perhaps sooner than he thought.

CHAPTER 2
BATTLES

Theodore Sullivan stroked his silver-gray mustache pensively. He wished it wasn't necessary to do what he had to do, but that was out of his control. He'd made promises, and he had to make sure they were fulfilled. There were ways. If only his daughter would listen.

Mulish little heifer. She'd always taken after her mother. He cherished her and hated her for it. But today, neither emotion was playing on his heartstrings. Today was strictly business. She'd understand that. Like her mother before her, she'd never been the typical emotional, fretful, helpless woman who seemed to be the norm in Victorian society. No, not her. She was more like a wild mustang filly. Testy, brazen, and as fully aware of her own mind as she was of her place in society. Well, today she would have to know her place.

He drew rein on the handsome palomino gelding he rode. The horse stopped on the top of a ridge, and Sullivan gazed down on the ranch below. It was a sight to behold. His son-in-law, Blake Bennet, was barely five years younger than Sullivan and it was clear he had spent his years carefully amassing a fortune. And making invaluable connections.

The valley was ranged entirely by Bennet cattle, bearing the back-to-back B brand, with not a homesteader in sight. Few ranchers managed that without resorting to violence, but somehow Blake Bennet had. The ranch house and outbuildings were immaculate, sprawling stone buildings. A lush garden surrounded the house and first-class horses grazed peacefully in the corrals, their well-combed tails swishing flies off their fat, gleaming rumps.

A thrill of satisfaction filled Sullivan. Yes. He'd made the best deal of his life when he married off his daughter to the richest, savviest rancher in the territory. Mentally patting himself on the back, he put heels to the palomino, a gift from his son-in-law, and the horse trotted obediently toward the homestead below. Moments later, Sullivan entered Bennet's study.

"How are you today, Blake?" he asked expansively, flashing his son-in-law a smile.

Blake looked up from a ledger book he was filling out and nodded in acknowledgement of his father-in-law's greeting, but he didn't return the smile. "I've been better," Bennet said. He was an imposing hulk of a man, taller than most and broad in the shoulders. His blue-gray eyes reminded Sullivan of gunmetal. Hard, unyielding and dangerous. His pitch-black beard and wavy black locks were clipped and shaped to perfection, slicked down with hair cream. His demeanor was one of underlying brutality. He was not a man to be crossed.

"I'm sure you'll come out on top again, whatever it is," Sullivan said confidently, depositing himself into a chair opposite the big man's desk. "An outfit like yours ain't easily sunk."

"Oh, it ain't my outfit sinking," Bennet returned, still unsmiling. "It's me getting mighty antsy."

Sullivan pressed his fingertips together and gave the nod of solemn contemplation and undivided attention that he knew the statement required, without probing for an elaboration.

"I ain't aiming to flog any dead horses, you understand, Theo, but your daughter ain't given me an heir yet. When I die, this all goes to her, and I ain't fixin' to give all my hard-earned riches to some woman who never did the one job she was meant to do." An edge of irritation laced Bennet's voice.

Sullivan winced inwardly. This was exactly what he'd been meaning to talk to his daughter about. Not a moment too soon, apparently. "She's been to the doctor, yes?" he said, trying to steer the conversation toward potential solutions rather than camping out on the problem and getting Bennet's dander up.

"Yeah. The old quack gave her a bunch of herb potions, ordered bed rest." Bennet harrumphed disgustedly. "Bed rest. My ma and her ma before her gave birth out in the fields. Women are all turning soft these days."

"Well, it's worth trying anything, I suppose. If it'll get you an heir, who cares how soft the woman is, right?" Sullivan tried another smile.

Bennet regarded him with narrowed eyes. "Yeah. I reckon there's a mite of truth in that."

"Don't you worry, I'm sure she'll deliver an heir for you soon. 'Never give up' is what I always say."

Bennet eyed him dubiously. "Never is a long time and time ain't on our side. The clock's ticking. Chances are getting slimmer every day that goes by. I've decided to give it another month."

Sullivan didn't ask what would happen after that month was up, if his daughter wasn't yet in the family way. It was better not to lead the imagination of people like Bennet down such paths. Besides, Sullivan had his own plans. Plans that would leave no need for an answer to that question. "Speaking of which, is my daughter around?" he asked. "I'd like a word with her privately."

"Last I saw, she was in the parlor," Bennet said dismissively, turning his attention back to his ledger books.

"Thank you," Sullivan said, rising from his seat.

He found her in the parlor just as Bennet had said, painting a color portrait of a young Indian man from a black and white photograph.

"Are you trying to insult your husband, woman?" Sullivan said, bitter distaste and revulsion rising in him.

His daughter simply looked at him, her eyes calm and a trifle sad but completely composed. "The Indian Wars are over, Father. Folks in the east are curious about the vanquished tribes, now. Surely you know such art will fetch handsome prices at the auctions."

Sullivan huffed. She knew him too well. No matter. There were more important things for him to spend his time on. He ignored her silver-tongued jibe and sat down on a nearby chair, motioning to her to do the same. "There is the matter of your childless state. We need to discuss it."

She looked at him, the familiar stubbornness kindling in her hazel eyes, but she sat down, folding her paint-stained hands in her lap and sitting straight-backed and stiff-necked in the chair beside his. "You know as well as I, there is nothing to be done, Father. How could there be when the fault is not with me, it's with..."

"Yes," Sullivan cut in sharply, glancing at the doorway of the parlor. "*We* know that, and that's how it will stay. Do you understand?"

"Yes. I understand, Father. I understand very well." Her tone conveyed more meaning than her words alone suggested.

"Good," Sullivan said. "Now, it's time you made work of getting with child, or you'll lose your easy lifestyle."

"It's hardly easy," his daughter retorted, her light brown curls bouncing as she jerked her chin up, her eyes flashing. "I work my fingers to the bone, and I hate the man I'm married to."

Sullivan's hand shot out and struck her rebellious cheek, flinging her head violently sideways. Her hand flew to the already reddening skin. There were no tears in her eyes when she looked back at him. Simply defiance. What would it take to break her spirit?

"You selfish, ungrateful hussy," Sullivan hissed. "I rescued you from that Neanderthal and his lice-infested village and arranged for you to marry the richest, most powerful rancher in the territory! You can have anything your fickle heart desires, all you need to do is ask. All *I'm* asking of *you* is to get yourself pregnant to keep your husband happy, and that's too much for you? Do you want him to go looking for another wife who can give him an heir? Do you want to be a divorcée?"

"That would be better than selling myself like some calico queen, just to keep the two of you happy. In fact, I'd rather be dead."

Her chin was up in the air again, and Sullivan knew a second slap would do nothing to lower it. In ranching, horses this obstinate usually ended up as dog meat. Sometimes such an end was unavoidable. "Tread lightly, my dear," he said, rising slowly from his chair while he held her gaze in his own cold stare. "You might just get your wish."

WALKS WITH BEARS felt more alive than he could remember feeling in a long time. The Pawnee were giving it their all, but he and his fellow dog soldiers were holding their ground.

All his senses were absorbed in the battle, the screaming

and yelling of men, the dust and sweat and blood, the weight of his tomahawk in his one hand and the sturdy handle of the broad-bladed, razor-sharp bowie knife in the other.

A Pawnee man charged him from the left, blasting obscenities in his own language. Walks With Bears was ready for him, pretending to move to the right. The man raised his left hand, getting ready to strike with a short sword, probably supplied by the White coyotes he belonged to.

Walks With Bears waited for the last possible moment, then he ducked to the left, slashing the blade of his tomahawk across the warrior's midriff. The man's tirade turned to a scream, his left hand arcing uselessly through the space Walks With Bears had only just evacuated. As the Pawnee man fell, Walks With Bears raised his right hand with the knife and plunged its full length into the base of the other man's neck.

The scream was stifled with a gasp and a gurgle. The warrior fell with a dull thud at Walks With Bears's feet and lay motionless. There was no time to celebrate. Another man was already rushing him.

The fools. Surely, they knew the dog soldiers' reputation? Surely they knew that being restricted by the buffalo skin sash, decorated with beads, feathers, and porcupine quills, would do nothing to diminish the killing capacity of a dog soldier? Were they simply looking to die in a blaze of glory? For the sake of what? They were nothing but hired dogs, the White man's pets. Useful only for betraying their own kind.

Walks With Bears steadied himself, his feet splayed apart, his back hunched, ready for the impact. Again, waiting for the last moment, he raised his right hand, pointing the knife straight forward. The warrior ran right into it, the blade splitting his heart in two. Walks With Bears brought the back of the tomahawk down on the man's skull. Bone crunched under the onslaught, and the man crumpled.

The dog soldier looked up, his eyes darting all around him, his ears alert for the sound of footsteps or grunting breaths, but the Pawnee seemed to retreat. His eye caught one man creeping up on Walks With Bears's friend, Rides The Sun. Without so much as a thought passing through his mind, Walks With Bears raised his tomahawk and threw it.

The Pawnee lifted a spear. As it reached full height, the tomahawk hit him in the back of his head, splitting it like a ripe melon. The man didn't even scream. The spear pegged into the ground behind Rides The Sun, and its owner fell against it, his body twitching in last convulsions.

For a while, a deathly silence reigned. The dog soldiers waited, their senses alert, watchful, waiting. They did not assume that a battle was over until there was confirmation from scouts. Then the cry came.

"The Pawnee dogs are running back to their masters with their tails under their bellies!"

A collective whoop of victory rose from the victorious warriors. Walks With Bears raised his hands, but no sound came from his lips. In the settling dust of the early morning skirmish, he saw into the spirit world, and what he saw gripped his heart with a pain he had covered over with rage for many long years.

A White woman stood in front of him, her soft brown curls framing her porcelain features, her hand reaching out to him, a soft smile on her full, coral lips. She held a baby on her hip, a dark-skinned boy, dressed in traditional Cheyenne clothing, just as his mother was.

"Wally!" her voice echoed all around him, though her lips did not move. "Wally, come to us!"

Pain seared his chest like a hot knife raking through muscle, bone, and sinew. Love and hate fought like lion and bear in his mind. Longing and disgust battled for dominance in his heart.

"My brother does not take the scalps he fought for," a deep voice said beside him. "My brother sees past the things he looks at."

The vision faded and Walks With Bears turned his head slowly in the voice's direction, like a man in a trance. "Rides The Sun is right," he said, the warm, heavy sensation of his friend's hand on his shoulder bringing him slowly back to the world of the living.

Rides The Sun pulled the arrow out of Walks With Bears's dog rope. Freed from the self-imposed restriction, Walks With Bears went about taking the scalps he had earned, but his heart was heavy. The vision had left his eyes but not his spirit. He could still hear her voice calling to him. "Come to us!"

What did it mean? Had she not deserted him? Chosen to follow the ways of her own people? Denied him the privilege that every father cherishes, the privilege of watching his son grow into a man? And yet the yearning he had always felt for her had not left him. He could not hate her, though he had, for more winters than he could count, hated her kind. Her people had taken her from him, her and their child.

Where did the vision want him to go? He did not even know if she and their child were alive or dead. He knew he was not ready to cross over to the camp of the dead. It was not his time. Of that he was certain. Did that mean she was still alive? Was the vision calling him to her? Perhaps she needed him?

A sudden, heavy gratitude filled him that this last battle had not been against White men. The Pawnee they had encountered were a band of scouts Walks With Bears knew had been tracking his group of dog soldiers in order to find out where they were and ambush them. As it was, the Pawnee were, as usual, full of themselves and had decided they would attack on their own, thinking Walks With Bears's party to be a small one and easily overpowered.

Normally, such thoughts would have filled Walks With Bears with a glowing sense of satisfaction. Not now. As he vaulted aboard his black warhorse, he felt only emptiness. Living on hatred and revenge hadn't made him happy. It hadn't healed his pain. What he wanted most of all was to obey the call of that vision. But how? Where to look?

Rides The Sun rode up alongside him as the band headed for one of their hideouts, zigzagging along rock ridges and down creeks in order to conceal their tracks in case any Pawnee survivors took it into their heads to tell their White masters of their crushing defeat and lead them to the packet of dog soldiers.

"Hollow Owl plans a raid on the White men tonight, at the place called Fountain," Rides The Sun said, his voice full of excitement. "They have a lot of good meat. We will eat well. Our families, too."

Walks With Bears gave his friend a long, hard stare. At any other time before, he would have eagerly joined in such a venture. The White man's rations were not enough. Their great White chief's promises unfulfilled, as usual. But he could not seem to ignite the fire in his heart that he needed. All he knew was that they must attack no White people that night. "No raids tonight," he said. "We will hunt."

"But there is hardly any game left," Rides The Sun protested, his voice full of confusion at his friend's unexpected response.

"Hardly any is not none," Walks With Bears said flatly. "We will hunt."

"You are our leader, and we will follow you, but I think it is foolishness what you do. Our people are starving while the White men eat fat cows. The White men who killed all the buffalo and left them to rot on the plains. The White men who murdered our people at Sand Creek." Rides The Sun's voice was low but passionate.

Walks With Bears held up his hand. "Do you tell me the history of our people I already know? Save your breath, Rides The Sun. Why, I do not know, but the spirits tell me we must not raid tonight. We will hunt. Tell Hollow Owl and the others."

Rides The Sun rode off, muttering to himself. Walks With Bears knew they would do as he instructed. At least for a few days. He sent up a prayer to the Great Spirit, Maheo, to provide an elk or some such large animal.

Again, the vision rose in his memory. "Wally! Come to us!"

He stifled a roar of pain and longing, turning it to a guttural groan in his throat as he slumped over his horse's withers and silently wept.

CHAPTER 3
CHOICES

Zeke caught Jessie watching him with that questioning look on her face again. Before she opened her mouth to speak, he knew what was coming.

"You goin' to tell us what's eatin' ya?" She slapped a ladleful of oatmeal into his bowl, followed by a chunk of butter.

"Ain't nothin' eating me," Zeke grumbled, stirring the oatmeal with his spoon and reaching for the honey pot.

"Well, now, that's not what it looks like," Jessie went on, unperturbed. "You been moonin' around here better than a week, ornery as a bear with a sore tooth, and you want me t' think there ain't nothin' eatin' ya?"

"Yeah, that's what I want you t' think," Zeke said, his eyes riveted on the honey as it dribbled into his food. He didn't really have an appetite. He was hungry, and that was the only reason he ate. He hardly tasted anything anymore.

"I'll thank ya to talk to my wife with a respectful tongue in your head," Tanner said, his voice gentle but firm.

"Yes, sir, Pa-Tanner," Zeke said, feeling his neck grow hot.

They'd been nothing but good to him for nigh on a decade, and he knew he was acting ungrateful. He truly wasn't ungrateful, though. He knew there was nothing he could do to earn the home they had given him, the care and the acceptance. Even the discipline. Every reprimand came from a place of wanting the best for him, wanting him to be the best he could be. They believed in him.

Strange that. They believed in him, when he didn't even believe in himself. How could he? How does a man believe in something when he doesn't even know what it is? How does a man believe in himself, when he has no idea who he is?

"You going to spit it out, or must I shake it out of you?" Jessie wasn't letting it lie.

Zeke sighed inwardly. There were some things he couldn't share with her. As much as he would like to. She wouldn't understand. As rough and ready as she was, she was still a woman. He had no doubt that she loved him, but he couldn't expect her to understand him.

"Maybe me and Zeke'll just take us a long ride out along the creek this morning," Tanner said.

Zeke looked up at him. Had the man read his mind?

"Well, I sure hope that helps to straighten out his face. I sure can't hold much longer with him, techy as a teased snake, he is." She peered under her eyebrows at Zeke, and he felt a chuckle rumble in his throat, as moody as he still felt.

"Won't hurt to try, I reckon," Zeke said, shoveling in the rest of his oatmeal. The kitchen was suddenly suffocating him. That ride along the creek was just what he needed.

After breakfast, with the sun just breaking past the horizon, Zeke and Tanner saddled up their horses and headed for Fountain Creek. There was a cottonwood forest a few miles up from the Nugent homestead, and it was here they dismounted and turned the horses loose to graze. Zeke lay down on his back along a fallen cottonwood trunk and stared up into the waving, shimmering leaves. The fluffy white seeds of the cottonwoods were falling, like lazy snowflakes, covering the ground.

"You recall the day that stranger rode through and I beat him in a quarter mile race?" Zeke said, aware that Tanner was waiting quietly on the end of the tree trunk he lay on.

"Sure do. You and Hoedown taught him a thing or two," Tanner said.

"You recall what he called me?"

Tanner hesitated a moment. "I reckon most of us didn't pay him any mind. I'll own I forgot. Wasn't more than a fool's raving, far as I'm concerned. And a sore loser at that."

Zeke sat up, blowing some cottonwood fluff away from his face. "You and Jessie, maybe, but I ain't sure about the rest of the town." He tried to keep his tone neutral, controlled, but he could already hear it rising.

"Now, I can't speak for other folks personally—" Tanner began, but Zeke cut him short.

"I seen it, Pa! They look at me different, now. That feller made 'em see things they didn't see before. All they knew was Zeke, the Nugents' kid. Now every time they look at me, they see them dog soldiers that killed folks and burned down crops and all. Dancing with Lucy the other night was like dancing with a wooden doll. One of them marionettes we seen when the traveling theater came through."

"Even if that is so, doesn't mean you have to start acting different when other folks start acting different around you. You decide who you are, nobody else," Tanner said calmly, chewing on a shaft of grass.

Zeke lay down again, his heart heavy. "That's just it, Pa. I don't know who I am. I don't feel right in my own skin no more."

"What's your meaning?" Tanner asked, his voice still calm.

"When I lived with the Nez Percé, I knew I looked different

to 'em, but it didn't matter much. When they beat the drums for their war dances, I felt like those drums became my own heart. Living on the Snake River, catching trout and picking nuts and berries, it was all I needed. I ain't never been happier."

An oriole flitted about in the trees above him, chirping and warbling, its mustard yellow chest fluffing out with each hop from branch to branch. Tanner waited silently for Zeke to continue.

"Then the White hunters came. The word around camp was that they were accusing us of stealing from the emigrants. Then a wagon train got raided one night, and their menfolk decided it was us, the Nez Percé. We were just minding out own business, and the next thing they came down on us, rifles blazin'. Me, I was down at the river, checking my fish traps. All I heard was shootin' and screamin'."

He paused. The memory of the horror made his chest ache and his muscles feel weak, his bones like wax.

"By the time I got back to the village, they were all dead. All of 'em. Every one."

The oriole chirped and warbled. The cottonwood leaves shuddered in the breeze. A fresh shower of fluff drifted down onto Zeke's face.

"I went looking for them White folks, the hunters. Couldn't find 'em. Like as not, they'd lit out of there already, headed for their promised land." He tried to hold back the bitterness, but he could still hear it in his own voice. "After that, well, I figured it was just me. I'd have to watch out for myself or die. Then I came here, and I figured I'd found a place to belong. Until now. It's all a lie, ain't it, Pa-Tanner? I ain't White and I ain't Indian. I'll never fit in nowhere, so what's the use of trying?"

"I don't hold so much with the idea of a fella being his tribe. I reckon every one of us got to find out who we are, ourselves. You got to find out who you are inside. The outside of you is just the wrapping." Tanner sat absentmindedly whittling a twig he'd picked up from the forest floor.

"But you know who your pa is, don't ya? And your ma?"

"Yeah, I do," Tanner began, looking like he wanted to clarify his statement, but Zeke went on.

"And so does Jessie. You know where you came from. The way I see it, a feller's got to know where he comes from before he can know where he's going."

"Hmmm..." Tanner said. The oriole fluttered off, chattering away. "So what do you think you've got to do? What d'ya think'll help you figure out who you are?"

The words spilled from Zeke's mouth without him thinking them through, or even thinking them at all. It was as if they came straight from his soul, his very spirit. "I got to go find out who my ma and pa are. The Nez Percé told me an old feller sold me to 'em for a slave when I was just a bitty baby. And I had this on my wrist." Zeke sat up and hooked a finger under his collar, pulling out a small medicine bag hanging round his neck on a rawhide thong. He opened it and fiddled inside before locating what he wanted. He pulled it out carefully and placed it in his palm. "Take a look," he invited Tanner.

The older man reached out and took the small, silver bracelet. It was made of chain links with a single silver plate about two inches long and a half inch wide. Tanner read the fine engraving on the plate and handed it back. "Elizabeth Sullivan," he said. "That your ma?"

"I reckon so."

"How come you never told us any of this?" It was an honest question. There was no recrimination in Tanner's voice or his eyes.

"I figured if she sold me, she didn't want me. I only figured out how to read this a long time after the Nez Percé were killed, and I'll own I don't know why I kept it. I wanted to hate her and the old man who sold me, but now I want to know who they are. I want to know what happened. I want to know who I am, Pa-Tanner."

"I reckon you do." Tanner nodded slowly, still chewing ruminatively on the grass stalk in his mouth. "Good luck telling Jessie that."

Despite the gravity of the conversation, Zeke had to smile. "I always been able to twist her arm."

"You sure have, but I've got me a notion it might not be so easy this time around." Tanner chuckled, then his eyes grew grave again. "I can't stop you, Zeke. I ain't of a mind to, neither truth be told. A fella's got to do what he figures is the right thing. The only one who knows your mind is you, and you got to sleep with your decisions every night."

Zeke held his adoptive father's gaze for a few moments longer. Tanner stood up and stepped closer. He gripped Zeke's hand and helped him to his feet, then he pulled him closer for a big, fatherly bear hug. Zeke fought off tears of guilt and frustration. It should be enough, what these two selfless people had given him. He should be satisfied with the family he had, the legacy they were giving him of their own free will.

But something inside him wouldn't rest. He'd had that recurring dream again, two nights in a row. It was like there was a call going out, becoming more and more urgent as time passed.

"Where'll you start looking?" Tanner asked as he drew away and walked over to his horse, Trigger.

"Well, I got my mother's name. Reckon I'll go to Denver. Take a gander at the state records. Might get me on the right track."

"Sounds like a fine idea," Tanner agreed, although he looked a little reluctant. "You want me to go with you?"

It was a tempting proposition. All his years of riding alone hadn't made Zeke any more fond of it than any other man might be. Zeke shook his head. "I reckon this is something I got to do alone. I can't take you away from the ranch, nor from Jessie. She needs you more."

Tanner looked like he understood. He just had to, that was all. Besides, it was high time Zeke started making his own way. He was twenty-one already. Well, according to the birthday Jessie had given him.

When they got back to the homestead and Zeke told Jessie his plan, she put both hands on her hips and gave him her muliest level stare. "You'll do no such thing, Ezekiel Nugent," she said, her tone unrelenting. "We're a family. We'll go to Denver together and we'll figure this out."

"You know I can't take you folks along with me," Zeke said, steeling himself for the storm of protest that his refusal would unleash.

"Don't think I ain't noticed how folks have changed since that no-good rider came through here and got himself beat by you and Hoedown," Jessie said, her eyes flashing. She pulled out a chair and sat down, patting the chair beside hers.

Zeke deposited himself in the chair and waited for the rest of her tirade.

Jessie stared him full in the eye. "I know what it's like when folks treat a body like they're less-than, just 'cause you don't fit their idea of what you should be like. I also know you're different, Zeke. Known it since the first day I met you. Other folks see it, too, but they don't cotton to it. I don't want you livin' that same hell I did, fightin' for yourself, makin' your own way in a world that won't give ya the time of day, not on any side of the tracks."

Zeke nodded. How to make her understand? "It's too late, Ma-Jess," he said, taking her hand and gripping it tight in both his own. "Folks already ain't givin' me the time of day. I got this to do and I got to do it on my own. It's the only way I'll be able to make peace with myself."

"We could just ride along, just till you've got a good strong lead," Jessie tried again, but Zeke could see that she understood, as much as she didn't want to.

He shook his head. "I'll be leavin' right away. With your blessin', I hope."

"Well, then." Jessie got up from her chair. "If you're so bound and determined, I won't stand in your way." She leaned her hands on the top slat of the ladder-back chair. "But so help me, if you get too independent for your own good and I find out you got in a scrape and didn't come back to us for help, I'll tan your hide, big as you are, you hear me?"

"I reckon you *would* whup me, ma'am, given half a chance," Zeke said, unable to hold back his smile.

Jessie's face softened, her eyes glistening in the midmorning sunshine filtering through the lace curtains of her kitchen. She stepped over to a cupboard in the corner and took out her gun belt. The two LeMats Zeke knew so well hung snugly in their holsters, the hammers neatly tied down with rawhide thongs. Jessie was nothing if not careful with six-shooters. "Here," she said, holding out the gun belt to Zeke. "You'd better take these. They're handy. And you'll be needing 'em more than I will."

Zeke stared at her. He knew what those guns meant to Jessie. He'd heard her tell the story of how she'd won them in a card game from a drunken Confederate soldier. How she'd carried them with her, and they'd been all that saved her life more than one time. "I... I can't take 'em, Ma-Jess," he said, tears pricking the back of his eyes.

"Sure you can," Jessie insisted, stepping closer with the gun belt. "It'll help me sleep better at night, knowin' you're well heeled." She thrust the gun belt into his hand.

Zeke took it, knowing if he didn't, it would be the greater

insult to her. He strapped on the belt, feeling the weight of the two powerful guns mirroring the weight of the burden on his soul. "I'll take good care of 'em," he said by way of a thank you.

Jessie nodded and brushed away a tear. "Then they'll take good care of you. Now get on out of here. Denver's waiting on ya and so are your folks."

She and Tanner helped him pack his saddlebags with provisions and Zeke mounted up, pressing his hat down low on his head. He hesitated for a moment, the reality of parting suddenly bringing home to him how much he saw these two people as his family. And here he was, riding off to find people he'd never seen or heard from before. People who might not want him. People who might prefer that he didn't even exist.

Zeke almost changed his mind right there, but somewhere off in the hills, a wolf howled, and the restlessness in his spirit returned. He didn't know anything for sure. And he wouldn't have peace until he knew. One way or the other.

Touching his fingers to the brim of his hat, he gave Jessie and Tanner one last nod in farewell and turned Hoedown's head north. He tried not to think too much about what he might find at the end of his journey. Better to keep his expectations low and his mind open. He might find himself out there on the trail, or he might lose everything he thought he had.

There really was no way of knowing, but he had it to do, and do it he would.

CHAPTER 4
DEAD ENDS

The offices of the courthouse clerk were quiet. An old man sat dozing in a corner of the waiting room. A single clerk doodled in a ledger book. Flies buzzed in the windows. Zeke walked over to the clerk's counter and cleared his throat.

The man looked up, squinting at him, then straightened a little and said in a lazy voice, "What's your business?"

"I'm looking for my..." Zeke began then changed his mind. "I'm looking for a lady, name of Elizabeth Sullivan."

The clerk stared at him blankly. An awkward silence followed. "You got any more information that that?" the clerk asked a trifle sarcastically.

"Uh, no." Zeke noticed the soft snoring from the old man in the corner had stopped.

"You know what city she's in?"

"If I did, I'd ride out there and find her myself," Zeke said, irritation rising in his throat.

"County, then? Area?"

"'Fraid not," Zeke said. "All I know is she lived round here. Denver City."

"And when was that?" the clerk asked.

"Maybe twenty years ago or so."

The clerk sighed.

A shuffling sound behind Zeke told him he was being approached. A moment later, the old man stood beside him, leaning against the clerk's counter.

"Did you say you're lookin' for a Sullivan? Elizabeth Sullivan?" the old man asked. His hair was white, his skin wrinkled and dry, his eyes pale blue and bloodshot but keen as a hawk's.

"Yeah, that's right," Zeke replied, immediately feeling cagey. "You know someone by that name?"

"Who's she to you?" the old man said, his eyes seeming to bore into Zeke's.

"She's..." He wanted to say *she's my mother,* but something held him back. "She's got information I need about my folks," he said instead.

"You a half-breed?" the man asked, his eyes narrowing even more.

"Even if I knew the answer to that, what's it to you, mister?" Zeke said coldly. The silver bracelet in his medicine bag seemed to be burning a hole in it, searing into his chest. He wanted to take it out and show them, show them that his search was legitimate, but instinctively he knew that would bring him more trouble than progress.

The old man stared at him a while longer, saying nothing.

Zeke held his gaze. "Pardon me, mister, but I'd like to carry on with my business. If you ain't got no vested interest in who or what I am or ain't, I'd be mighty obliged if you'd leave me in peace." He turned back to face the clerk. "You going to look up that name in the records or what?" he asked, barely keeping a handle on his anger. "Elizabeth Sullivan. S-U double L I-V-A-N."

"I can spell Sullivan," the clerk snapped. He sauntered over to a large cabinet and began rifling through boxes of papers, muttering under his breath.

The old man was still leaning against the clerk's counter beside Zeke. The man's stare made Zeke's hair stand up on the back of his neck, but he kept his eyes trained on the clerk who was still shuffling and muttering.

At last, the clerk straightened up and shoved the boxes back into place. "Nothing there," he said flatly.

"No Sullivans at all?" Zeke asked incredulously.

"You sayin' the feller's lyin'?" the old man said in a low tone.

Zeke turned his head to look at him, keeping his eyes shaded by his hat. "I'm sayin' I know she lived here. I'm sayin' I know her pa lived here. Maybe they still do. I'm sayin' it's mighty irregular that there's no records of 'em. I'm sayin' maybe we should dig a little deeper."

The clerk leaned both hands on the wooden surface of his counter. "I dug as deep as I need to," he said coldly. "There ain't no records for no Sullivans here."

Zeke looked from one to the other. Either they were lying, or his mother and her family had never registered themselves. He decided to try another tack. The local saloons. Barmen often knew more about a town and its history than the court records clerks did.

"Well, then, I reckon I'm wasting both our time, ain't I?" he said, turning on his heel and marching from the clerk's office. Out in the street, he looked around, aware that the two men inside were still watching him. He could feel their eyes on his back.

Unlooping Hoedown's reins from the hitching rail, he led the horse down the street. It was still early, and the streets were not much busier than the clerk's office. That was a good thing. The fewer people heard him talking to the barkeeps, the better. He stopped in front of the first saloon, the Curly Cactus Saloon.

Stepping inside, he let his eyes adjust to the shadowy interior and then stepped over to the long wooden bar counter at the one end of the room. A honky-tonk pianist was playing a lazy tune. A handful of old-timers lay about, one of them sleeping, others reading newspapers or staring into space.

"What'll it be, sonny?" a friendly, gravelly voice asked.

Zeke looked up into the bearded face of the barkeep. "Just a cider, thanks. With a side of information if you've got any."

The barkeep smiled. "I'll tell you everything you need to know," he said, fetching a glass from the glass shelf behind him and producing a bottle of pale-yellow liquid from an ice box below the counter.

Zeke paid for the drink, took a long swig and wiped his mouth with his sleeve. The action made him think of Jessie, and he wished for the space of two breaths that he'd brought her and Tanner along.

"What's it you're looking to find out, then?" the barman prompted.

Zeke had learned his lesson. He wasn't about to go being honest and asking direct questions again. He pondered for a moment, took another swig of cider and swallowed. "I've heard there's a mighty fine family around here called the Sullivans. You know 'em?"

The barman raised one eyebrow. "Know 'em? Heck, everybody knows 'em. You got a beef with 'em?"

Zeke paused, taking another sip of cider to stall for time. A beef with them? Funny that should be the first thing the barman thought of. "No, can't say I have. Why? Do most folks?"

The barman laughed. "Naw. It's just that old Mr. Sullivan, he's a real cagey feller. Keeps to himself more than not. Folks don't know much about him, just that he's real rich and he gets his way around town."

"So he lives here?" Zeke had to control his excitement. What a strange turn of events. First being completely stonewalled and then having information drop into his lap like ripe plums.

"Not in Denver."

"But close to Denver, yeah?"

"Who's askin'?" a voice cut in. One of the men who'd been dozing in a booth came and sat down beside Zeke at the bar.

"Just a saddle tramp, wanting a job. I figure if I can find a feller who's flush, I'll at least be sure of getting paid." It was a reflexive answer. He hadn't thought anything through. He hadn't expected that he'd need to make up stories.

"You don't look like a saddle tramp," the man said. "You look like a half-breed."

Zeke swallowed his retort and kept his silence.

"Take my advice," the man said, his eyes narrowed and mean. "You stay away from the Sullivans. They don't want your kind around. Sullivan'd sooner shoot you than hire you on, so don't even bother trying."

Zeke clenched his teeth. Jessie had been right. He was being prejudged left, right, and center.

As a child he hadn't come up against folks calling him a half-breed. He'd stayed hidden, shunned towns and settlements except to steal food and clothing from at night. In Fountain, he'd been the Nugents' boy. Now he was a stranger who looked half Indian. He'd have to grow scales like a desert lizard and let their words slide off him without leaving a mark, or he'd go out of his skin.

"Well, thanks for the information," he said.

The barman gave him a strange look, almost apologetic, then turned away and went to polishing glasses. Zeke downed the rest of his cider and set the glass down. He turned and left, aware that, once again, his every step out of the building was being watched.

He tried four more saloons that day, with no success. Every

time there was either a close-mouthed barman or someone else to tell him he had better lay off looking for anyone named Sullivan. By the fifth saloon, he began to realize he was drawing too much attention to himself. People were starting to stare at him in the street, some openly antagonistic, their eyes warning him away, letting him know he was not wanted, not welcome.

After a quick meal of kidney pie and potato salad at a café, he mounted up and rode out of town. Where he was going, he didn't know. All he knew was that he had to get out of Denver. It was like the town had spat him out like he had a foul taste.

A storm was brewing. Cold winds whipped around him, but he hardly felt them. Great, towering thunderheads grumbled and boomed. Lightning flashed as the clouds marched across the sky, and rain began to fall in fat drops. Spread out at first, then falling thicker and faster, until Zeke was riding through a deluge of water. Small rivers began to form around Hoedown's plodding hooves.

Zeke didn't even bother to pull out his slicker. He was wet through already. He simply let his horse navigate a path through the hills, keeping his rump to the wind.

After a while, the rain passed and a watery afternoon sun poked shafts of light between what was left of the shrinking, raggedy clouds. Zeke looked around him, not knowing where he was. Hoedown was picking his way along a ridge.

Hastily, he turned the horse down the slope a ways and stumbled upon a trail. The thought occurred to him that maybe he should go back. He still hadn't found his mother. He couldn't give up that easily. But an even stronger compulsion kept him moving eastward.

He could feel the warm sun on his back, and soon steam began to lift from his shirt and pants and from Hoedown's hide. East. Away from the setting sun. He had heard there were Indian reservations somewhere south of the Arkansas River.

Perhaps he should go looking there. Surely his own people would not look at him as if the cat had dragged him in. Surely, they would answer his questions.

But what about Elizabeth Sullivan? He had hit a brick wall, no doubt about it, but at least he had her name. He had no idea what his father's name was. Elizabeth would be able to tell him about his father, about his heritage. Without her, he had no idea where to look for his father. Then again, if she was anything like her father, chances of her telling him anything were slimmer than the chances of finding her to begin with, anyhow.

He'd never been as far as the Arkansas River. He had no idea how far it was. But he knew one thing. He was going there. He rode all the rest of that day and most of the night, using the stars to keep him headed in the right direction. He didn't follow a trail. Trails would be populated by men who would see the half-breed stranger, not the man inside.

When his eyes began to fall closed on their own, he stopped in a grove of aspens and hobbled Hoedown. Removing the saddle, he used it for a pillow and fell soundly asleep as soon as his head hit the leather. The dream came to him again, and before the sky had begun to turn gray, he woke with a start, every inch of him alert and ready.

By the time the sun crested the horizon, he had left the mountains behind and entered the flats, the Great American Desert, it was called. Though why they called it that, Zeke couldn't imagine. Sure, the trees thinned out to almost nothing, but there were plenty of water sources if you knew where to look, and long grass waving in the wind. Dotted about were small bushes, and around bushes there was always life.

His food lasted another four days. After that, he caught small game in traps, fished in the creeks he came across, and picked berries. He also dug for roots. It wasn't women's work when a man was alone and starving. After seven days, he lost count. The sun set and rose, set and rose, and Zeke kept riding toward the rising sun, the clutter in his mind seeming to blow away little by little in the sweeping prairie winds and icy, pelting rainstorms.

It could have been two or three weeks, maybe longer, before he stumbled upon the Indian Territories. Almost too late, he realized he looked too much like a White man to be safe among the tribes exiled there. He took off his hat and hung it on his saddle horn then pulled off his shirt, tying it around his waist before he entered the first village.

Curious children gathered round, staring at this strange mixture of White man and Indian. He tried to sign to them in the universal Indian sign language that Jessie had taught him, but they just giggled and covered their hands with their mouths. One of them ran off to call someone, and soon there were adults around him, pointing at him and jabbering to each other.

He tried to sign again. *I seek the Nez Percé. I come to ask questions of them about my father.*

He knew better than to take out the silver bracelet. It would be snatched up by a wide-eyed child in no time and it was unlikely he'd ever see it again.

A loud exclamation broke through the chatter of voices, and a tall, fierce-eyed man stepped through the crowd. They parted to let him through, making a wide path as if he was much respected and nobody wanted to get in his way. He stopped, staring hard at Zeke. Then he said something in his own language.

I seek the Nez Percé, Zeke signed again.

The man stopped, looking a little confused. Then he signed back. *Who is your father? Where do you come from?*

I do not know. It is what I have come to find out.

That meant something to the tall, fearsome man. He chased away the other villagers and motioned urgently to Zeke to dismount and follow him. Zeke did as he asked, hoping he was not in trouble. Those eyes had seen many battles, he could instinctively tell.

WALKS WITH BEARS was sharpening his weapons when he heard the excited chattering of the children. He smiled to himself. It was good when something out of the ordinary happened on the reservation. At least their minds were occupied for a while. Since the tribes had been forced to abandon their ancient ways, there had seemed little to do. Their usual daily rituals and chores had been replaced with the sedentary life of poor White farmers and beggars.

Walks With Bears shook off the depressing thoughts and went on honing his arrows and tomahawk to razor sharp edges while the hubbub died down. But all was not quiet then. Instead, he could hear Rides The Sun speaking animatedly, his voice growing louder as he approached Walks With Bears's tipi.

"He will not believe it. I do not believe it myself and I see you with my own eyes. It cannot be any other way. This is a great day, my friend, a great day!"

Walks With Bears looked up to see his old friend standing before him with a young man at his side. Rides The Sun was smiling, opening his arms and saying something, but Walks With Bears did not hear a word of it. His whole attention was riveted on the young man beside his friend. His tools and weapons fell to the ground at his feet.

Was it possible? And yet very little else seemed possible. He might as well have been looking into a still pool of water and seeing his younger self staring back at him, except that the man's hair was lighter and curlier than his. And cut short like a White man's. The young man looked as shocked as Walks With Bears felt.

"Hotohkôhma'aestse," he said hoarsely, whispering his son's name. The son he had thought was dead.

The young man began to sign, *I seek the Nez Percé. I wish to know who my father and mother are.*

"You know their names?" It could be coincidence. It might be that the resemblance was a fluke.

"Only my mother's name. I have this..." The young man broke off and opened the small medicine bag hanging from his neck. Pulling out a small, silver bracelet, he held it out.

Walks With Bears took it from him, his hands shaking. The silver plate was engraved with writing that he could hardly read anymore. Slowly he mouthed out the letters, remembering them one by one. She had taught him well, but he had not read the White man's letters for a long time.

"Elizabeth Sullivan," the young man helped his stumbling tongue in a hopeful voice.

Walks With Bears stared at the letters. Yes, that was what they said. "Lizzie," he whispered, a monsoon of longing, pain, and loss crashing over him. He fell to his knees in the dirt, clutched the bracelet to his chest, and let all the years of pent-up anguish rip through him in one raw, heartbroken cry.

CHAPTER 5
MEETING

Rides The Sun's hand pressed on Walks With Bears's shoulder. The latter opened his eyes to see the boots of the young man still there in front of him. The edge of the bracelet with Lizzie's name on it dug into his skin, he was gripping it so hard. Walks With Bears took a shaky breath and composed himself. He waited until his breathing was again even and measured before he spoke.

"I am Walks With Bears," he said in his best English, standing to his feet and looking into the young man's face. If his reading had deteriorated, at least he could still remember the spoken language. Or so it appeared.

"I am Zeke. Zeke Nugent," the young man said. He held out his hand and Walks With Bears grabbed Zeke's wrist in a firm grasp. The young man gasped and then followed Walks With Bears's cue. They stayed that way for a few moments. Walks With Bears felt like there were no words to speak and, at the same time, too many to say. Too many to know where to begin. If Zeke had any, he wasn't speaking them.

"Your mother named me Wally," he said, smiling sadly at

the memory, his eyes burning with unshed tears. "It is a White man's name, yes?"

Zeke smiled and nodded. "A White man's name. I think she took it from the sound of your name in the White man's tongue. Walk could change to Wally." He looked a little nervous. It was understandable.

Walks With Bears felt nervous too. Here was his own flesh and blood, and yet he was a complete stranger. "You come far?" Walks With Bears said. "You have eaten?"

Zeke shook his head. "I ain't eaten much in the last few days. Left Fountain around three weeks ago, if I was to make a wild guess."

"Fountain?"

"Yeah. It's a settlement near Colorado City."

"I know Fountain," Walks With Bears said shortly. He didn't tell Zeke how he knew it. He didn't tell him he and his dog soldiers had been planning a raid on the settlement when he saw the vision of his wife and son.

"You know Fountain?" Zeke asked, his voice becoming more excited. "How's that?"

It was a question Walks With Bears decided should go unanswered, for the time being at least. "We eat, then we talk," Walks With Bears said, rising to his feet. For a moment, he paused. His heart was full, but his son was a stranger to him. He could see the longing in the lad's eyes, the questions, the sadness. Time. They both needed time.

"I have fresh meat," Rides The Sun said. "I will cook it for us. You and your son talk alone until it is ready."

Zeke looked confused. Walks With Bears translated for him and Rides The Sun left for his lodge. Walks With Bears ushered his son past the open flap of his lodge and followed him inside. The young man stood, but not uneasily.

He seemed to know that it was considered respectful to wait

for his elder to tell him when to sit. Walks With Bears sat down on the far side of the fire and patted the buffalo robe beside him. Zeke came and sat down.

"You have questions," Walks With Bears said. He knew from experience that the best way to get a man talking was to find what it was he wanted to talk about. When he got that far, it was easy to steer him in almost any direction.

"Yeah, I do," Zeke said carefully.

"Then you must ask," Walks With Bears said, taking his long pipe and filling it with kinnikinnick. He took his time stamping down the dried leaves into the brightly painted bowl. "I answer what I know."

"First thing I want to know is where's my mother?" Zeke began.

Walks With Bears looked up sharply from his pipe. "She is not with you?" He had, all this time, assumed they would be together, his wife and his son. That was the natural order of things. No other possibility had entered his mind.

"No," the young man named Zeke replied. "I never knew her."

Confusion and anger flared up in Walks With Bears's heart. "She abandoned you too?"

"I don't know what happened," Zeke said, his features hard. "All I recollect is living with a family of settlers. They all had red or yellow hair and white skin with freckles. Not at all like me, so I knew I was not one of their family. They sold me to a village of Nez Percé as a slave. They needed supplies to get to Oregon. When I was about ten winters, my village was attacked by settlers. I was down at the stream, checking my fish traps, so I survived. I think I was the only one."

Walks With Bears longed to take his son in his arms and share his pain. If only he had ignored Sullivan. If only he had stolen his child back, the boy would have grown up in a village full of people who loved him. He would have had a happy childhood instead of believing himself an orphan.

"How long ago did you see my mother?" Zeke asked, his eyes earnest.

"You still wish to find her? After she gave you away?"

"I don't know that she gave me away. I don't know anything. I want answers. When I have them, I will decide what I want after that."

Walks With Bears sighed. It was a truth he had been avoiding. He had told himself for so many winters that he could not look for her without risking his own life, and that would be senseless. He had clung to the belief he should simply stay alive in case she came to look for him. But what if she had been waiting for him?

But there was nothing he could do to change the past. The least he could do was tell his son what he knew.

"Nineteen winters I have not seen her." He stopped. That was not entirely true. "Twenty winters," he corrected himself.

Zeke looked almost wounded, but he nodded in apparent acceptance of Walks With Bears's answer. "Can you remember the last place you saw her?"

Walks With Bears's chest felt like it was about to collapse. Breathing hurt. He didn't want to talk about it. He picked up a burning twig from the fire in the middle of his lodge and used it to light his pipe. Slowly, carefully, he drew the fire through the kinnikinnick with his breath, feeling the warmth of the smoke and tasting the woody musk fill his mouth.

"I think always of the first place I saw her," he said, feeling his tongue slowly warming to the shapes and sounds of the White man's language. "The last place I cannot remember."

Zeke sat silently for a while, staring at his knees, which he had drawn up and wrapped his arms around. Walks With Bears smoked just as silently. After a few puffs, he held out the pipe to his son.

"We smoke, then I tell you all I know."

Zeke took the clay pipe gingerly, looking as if he were afraid he might break it. Or perhaps he was afraid of the kinnikinnick inside it.

"This one is not strong. I mix many herbs. Not strong."

Zeke nodded and took a careful draw. He held the smoke in his mouth a moment then let it drift from his lips and his nose. He nodded and gave his father a slightly embarrassed smile as he handed the pipe back. Walks With Bears took another draw himself.

His mind could not take hold of the thought that this was his son, even though he looked like the ghost of Walks With Bears's younger self. He had felt sure, at one time, that Lizzie and their son must be dead. Since she had not come back after a winter, or two winters, or five winters. Surely, if she had really wanted to, she would find a way to come back to him.

At ten winters, he had decided they had either gone to one of the big waters or had both been killed. He'd made a precarious peace with the fact that he would see neither of them again, and yet there had always been a lingering sense of their presence with him, a faint hope that one day he would at least get a glimpse of who they had become.

He'd never imagined he would see his son face to face. He'd never imagined the boy would be the near spitting image of himself. It was all a little too much to take in. The look in Zeke's eyes seemed to convey the same emotion. Walks With Bears could tell he was taking time to assess the situation before he gave himself freely. That was wise.

"The first time I saw your mother, she was riding with her father. Hunting. I see women hunt, I see them fight, I see them raid, but not White women. White women ride in coaches, wear long dresses, carry mushrooms made of cloth to keep the sun away from their skin.

"But your mother, she carried a gun, rode a horse, and shot game. I was scouting for her father, and so I saw her many times after that. One day she asks me to show her my village and teach her the language and customs of my people. I ask her, 'Why do you wish to know all this?' She says, 'Because the more we know about people, the better we can understand them and live in peace together.' So I showed her everything. Soon we knew that we cannot live apart any longer. We are one spirit in two bodies."

Walks With Bears paused, taking another drag on the pipe. Zeke crossed his legs and leaned forward, clearly absorbed in the story.

"We decided to marry. But her father said no. I brought him ponies, ten ponies, the same price for a chief's daughter. He still said no. He shot at me and chased me away with much shouting, ponies and all. I told Lizzie—your mother—we will elope. I will steal her in the middle of the night. My mother was not happy. She said our people will not look on me with favor. She said it will bring bad medicine to steal my bride. But I cannot do anything else. I love Lizzie. Lizzie loves me."

The young man named Zeke was watching him closely as he spoke. There was pain in his eyes. The pain of no answers and many questions. Walks With Bears knew that pain. He still had no answers and too many questions himself. He wondered how he would be able to give his son any answers if he did not have any for his own questions.

"We were married in my mother's lodge. Lizzie's father did not come to see us. The summer went back to the south and the winter came down from the north. Lizzie told me she is with my child. When the snow was all gone from the mountains, our baby was born. A boy. He was beautiful and strong. But then one night I rode out with a hunting party. When I came back, I found Lizzie is gone. Our baby is gone."

Walks With Bears stopped again. Telling the next part would be nigh on impossible. He knew the young man watching him would want to know everything, but it would have to wait. He would have to be patient. Walks With Bears got up and went outside. Moments later, the young man joined him.

"We eat," Walks With Bears said, pointing to Rides The Sun's lodge. The young man nodded, and they walked in silence to the painted buffalo skin tipi. The smell of roasting meat would have made Walks With Bears's mouth water on any other day. Today he had no appetite.

Ducking inside the lodge, they joined Rides The Sun. He served up the deer meat with some soup stewed from the bones, to which he had added fragrant herbs and fleshy roots. The young man ate hungrily. Walks With Bears watched him, barely touching his own food.

When the young man was done, he looked up expectantly, wiping his mouth on the deep blue cloth around his neck. "Wally, ah, Walks With Bears, did you go looking for Lizzie?" he asked.

Walks With Bears looked down. He shook his head. "No more my eyes saw Lizzie. No more they saw my son. They are gone. Vanished like the mist over the river when the sun burns hot."

The young man Zeke looked disappointed. "But what did you do? Did you look for them, us, at least?"

Walks With Bears stared out of the open flap of his friend's lodge, avoiding his son's eyes. "I swore revenge on the White man who stole my wife and my son from me. I joined Chief Tall Bull and the dog soldiers, and we fought the Whites. We fought even harder after the army killed the Peace Chief Black Kettle and his whole village."

He knew his voice was hard and edgy, but he could not change it. His heart would not let him.

"I fought for Lizzie. I fought for our son. I had much hate in my heart. I wanted to hate her, but I could not. So, I hated the people she came from and left me for." He lowered his voice. "But then, about eight winters ago, I saw a vision of Lizzie. In her arms she held a young child. In the vision she tells me to come to her, to our son. After that, no more raids. No more stealing. No more burning. I decided to fight only when the White man fights first."

He sighed. "And now the fighting is no more. We are in this place, this place that is not our lands, where we are told to live in peace with our ancient enemies. They call it a reservation, but they do not tell us what that means. They say we can live our old way of life, but that is a lie. There is nothing to hunt, nowhere to go, nobody to fight. We do women's work and sit in our lodges and grow weak and lazy. The fire water makes our old men forget who they are and makes our young men old and their minds like children's. We have no more honor, no glory. No freedom."

Walks With Bears looked up. His son was staring at him.

"But you did not come here to hear this. I am sorry. I cannot give you the answers you seek."

The young man's eyes were wide, pleading, desperate. "Please, try to remember where she was the last time you went to fetch her. I must know what happened. Please. Where did her father live? Even just the town, I will go look for her myself."

Walks With Bears felt his throat constrict. This was a son he could be proud of. But he was asking him to drag up memories that were too painful.

"Please, Walks With Bears," Zeke said. "Please... Father."

When Walks With Bears spoke again, his voice cracked. "Sullivan had a ranch toward the rising sun from the town called Booneville. If it is still there, I do not know."

"East of Booneville? That's near Pueblo, ain't it?"

"Yes. Pueblo."

"I'll leave right now."

"No. You will stay a few days," Walks With Bears said. "You need strength for the journey back."

"I'll be fine," the young man was impatient. He began to rise to his feet.

"I am your father and I wish to know my son a little better before Sullivan has a chance to murder him."

Zeke sank back down onto the buffalo robe, his eyes worried. "You think he'll do that?" he whispered.

"If a man tries to kill a father, why will the same man not try to kill that father's son?"

CHAPTER 6
CLOSE SHAVE

Walks With Bears's words sent a cold shiver down Zeke's spine. His father had clearly not told him the whole story. He wanted to ask more questions, but it seemed wiser to take the information he had and run with it. It was enough to know his grandfather had tried to kill his father. A man who was warned knew to tread lightly and prepare well.

"All right," he agreed after a few moments silence. "I'll stay a few days. But only enough to build up my strength."

Walks With Bears nodded and looked pleased. Zeke didn't say so, but he was glad his father had insisted he stay. He wanted to know him a little better, too, before he went looking for his mother.

In the days that followed, Walks With Bears showed Zeke their village and introduced him to the other tribe members. He showed him their corn fields and the beef cattle. The land was good, but Zeke could tell the men were mere shadows of their former selves. He'd seen the nations when they roamed freely over the prairies and mountains.

They were built for freedom, for wide open spaces, for

tracking and hunting and living close to the heart of nature. Settling dulled their senses. It made their bones weak, and their minds restless. All at once he knew why he himself had always felt that way, as if he were suffering perpetually from cabin fever.

In the many hours they spent together, Zeke told his father his full story. How he had grown up with the Nez Percé, learned to fish, hunt, and track. He told him of his wandering years as a lonely, frightened child. The short stint he'd sought a father figure in a criminally minded cattleman and eventually found a home with Jessie and Tanner Nugent, who had given him their name and loved him like their own son.

Walks With Bears told his son many tales of Cheyenne life in a village near the Arkansas river, the battles he had taken part in, as well as the raids. He was brutally honest and ended with an admonition that his son should not be as foolish as he had been.

"Anger is not your friend, Zeke," Walks With Bears said after a long silence around the fire one night. "Anger is a liar. It tells you it will give you strength, but it makes a man weak. It is a weak man who destroys everything around him that he does not understand."

Zeke watched the light of the flames dancing on his father's skin. Walks With Bears had painted both their faces with war paint that afternoon, at his son's insistence, and it gave the older man's face an otherworldly aspect. It took Zeke back to the nights around the fire with the Nez Percé. He had felt most at home with them, although he had been a slave to the family that traded four buffalo hides and a horse for him.

The next morning, Walks With Bears woke him well before sunup. Zeke came immediately awake the moment his father's hand touched his shoulder.

"You will go now," Walks With Bears said simply.

Zeke nodded and rose without comment. He washed himself, dressed in his Western clothes again, and saddled up Hoedown. When he hit the trail, his saddlebags were full of provisions: nuts, dried berries, dried beef made much like pemmican, and flat cakes his father called fry bread.

"I'll be back soon as I can, Ného'e," Zeke said, using the Cheyenne word for father as he mounted up onto Hoedown.

Walks With Bears smiled and patted his son's knee. His eyes seemed misty. "I wait for you," he said.

Zeke had the sense his father didn't put much store in him finding anything good to report. It made him that much more determined to find his mother and know the truth. Had she willingly given him up? Had she willingly left her husband's side and gone back to her people?

This time, Zeke knew exactly where to go and the ride was shorter, though only by a few days. When he reached Booneville, it was coming onto evening, and Zeke decided to make camp outside of town. He found a spot near the river that was well protected by an embankment and a grove of hackberry trees. They were full of fruit but not yet ripe.

Settling down on his bedroll with his saddle for a pillow, Zeke stared up at the darkening sky and munched on the last of the dried hackberries his father had added to his saddlebags. He let the fire burn down to coals and roasted the last of the fry bread and a hare he had shot along the way. It would be better not to stoke up the flames again. He didn't want to announce his presence before he was ready.

That night, Zeke slept fitfully. He kept dreaming of voices calling out to him. Whose they were and where they were coming from, he did not know. Frequently he awoke with a start, lying dead still and listening. All he could hear was the chirp of crickets and the rumble of thunder from far across the prairie. When dawn came, he was already lying with his eyes wide open, waiting for the light to make it possible to rise and take care of his morning routine.

When he was washed up and had breakfasted on nothing but coffee, Zeke mounted up and rode into town, taking his time. His entire morning operation had been a leisurely affair. He wanted to create the impression that he was nothing more than a saddle tramp passing through. Riding into town at the crack of dawn would not have done much to promote such an image.

He headed for the saloon first, went inside, and ordered a cup of Arbuckle's and a ranch breakfast of bacon, eggs, fried potato cakes, and fried tomatoes. He took his time over the meal, watching to see what the traffic was like in town. Satisfied that most folks seemed to be about their business and not frequenting the saloon, he struck up a conversation with the barkeep.

"There many ranchers round these parts?" Zeke asked once the obligatory introductions had been taken care of.

"A few," the barkeep said briskly. "You hunting a job?"

"That obvious, is it?" Zeke said, feigning embarrassment.

The barkeep laughed. "I see your kind in here all the time. Ain't nothing new to me."

"Well, if you could give me a name and point me in a direction, that'd be mighty topping of ya," Zeke said.

"Can't say I know who's hiring," the barkeep hedged.

"Well, maybe if I had a few names, I could ask around a bit," Zeke said lazily.

The barkeep paused. Then he picked up a notepad and pencil and came to sit down beside his only patron of the moment.

"There's the Morley ranch, out west of here." He scribbled on the notepad. "There's the Gordon ranch to the north, and the Leidermann ranch to the south." More scribbling. "Then there's the Bennet ranch out east."

Zeke took a swig of coal black coffee strong enough to float a colt in and waited for the barkeep to say something more, but the man was silent. "I heard there were Sullivans ranching here," he said. "They still in this valley?"

Immediately the atmosphere changed. "Nope. Just the ones I told you about. Might wanna steer clear of the Bennet place, now that I think about it. They've got all the hands they need, and Mr. Bennet, well, you won't like working for him." The barman stood to his feet. "That'll be four bits," he said, holding out his hand.

Zeke didn't need to ask whether he'd overstayed his welcome. He popped the last potato cake into his mouth and dug in his jeans pocket for the price of his breakfast. Then he gulped down the dregs of his coffee and plopped the coins into the barkeep's outstretched hand.

"Thanks. You've been mighty helpful, mister," Zeke said, scraping his chair back and replacing his hat on his head. Just to be sure he wasn't imagining the sudden change in the barman's demeanor, Zeke tossed one more stone in the bush. "You ever heard of a lady, name of Lizzie? Lizzie Sullivan? Lived around here with her pa?"

"You'd best be leaving, saddle tramp," the barman said, his lips thinning out into an uncompromising line. "Likely you'll have better luck out Pueblo way than around here." He walked away, shoving the coins into his pocket.

Zeke watched him go for just a moment. The barman had forgotten his notepad on the table, so Zeke tore off the first page with the names of the ranches scribbled on it and shoved it into his pocket. Then he stood up and left the saloon.

Something was off, and he wished he knew what it was. His grandfather was either a very private, reclusive man, or he was deeply disliked by all who knew him. Considering what Zeke's father had told him about Mr. Sullivan, neither possibility seemed improbable.

Zeke spent the rest of the day riding the trails and watching the ranches from afar. He'd forgotten one thing. His mother might have married someone else, so she wouldn't go by Sullivan anymore. She might not be on any of these ranches, or one of them might be her husband's. But he couldn't know that. She could be a Morley or a Gordon or a Leidermann. Maybe even a Bennet.

Or she could be a thousand miles back east. Or she could be on one of dozens of ranches all over the Midwestern territories. Or she could be pushing up daisies in some bone orchard some-where. He might find her tomorrow. Or he might spend the rest of his life looking for her.

These were the thoughts that trickled through his mind as he rode the hills, watching the ranch hands at work, scouting for the best vantage point from which to watch the ranch homesteads. Even if he did see his mother, he wouldn't know her. Perhaps the best thing to do was to simply ride in and ask. But the barkeep's kneejerk reaction to the mention of Lizzie Sullivan's name made him feel wary.

By late afternoon, he had determined that, of the four ranches, three had womenfolk who might be his mother's age, according to what Walks With Bears had told him. Gordon, Leidermann, and Bennet. All the ranches were well manned. Most of the men wore guns, but the Bennet ranch hands seemed to be most amply supplied with firearms.

Zeke made camp in a different place that evening and cooked his meal well before sundown, taking care to make a small smokeless fire to roast the dry and stringy but filling rabbit he had trapped earlier that day. Again, he camped not too far from the river, in a small gully populated with juniper and a few red cedar trees. With the fire burned down to coals once again, Zeke settled down behind a large, oblong-shaped, sun-warmed boulder and waited for sleep.

It seemed like he had only just dozed off when he came abruptly alert. The night was inky black all around him. What had woken him, he did not know. He knew better than to move around until he knew the answer to that question. It could be a rattler getting close for warmth, or a coyote looking for leftovers or easy pickings. Hoedown huffed restlessly. Zeke strained his ears.

There it was. A faint rustle of leaves, though the night was windless. A twig snapped. The sound of metal scraping against holster leather. Hoedown shifted his weight. A gun hammer clicked. Zeke pressed both hands against the boulder and counted silently in his head. *One, two, three...*

On three, he heaved against the boulder and rolled down the side of the gully just as flame stabbed into the black night above him and the report of the shot echoed out across the valley. Zeke landed on his haunches at the bottom of the gully, his right hand already palming a LeMat. He couldn't see much in the darkness, just the dark bulk of someone on top of the boulder.

Pulling off a shot, Zeke sprang immediately to his left, this time rolling down the length of the gully and behind another boulder. A hoarse, grating curse reached his ears. The scuffle of a hurried retreat followed. Hoof beats. Then silence.

Zeke stayed crouched where he was, waiting. He wasn't about to go anywhere until the crickets felt comfortable to go back to chirping. He waited for so long, his leg went to sleep, and he had to massage it for a few minutes after he straightened it out again, trying to stop the sharp needle-like pain that shot through skin and muscles as the blood circulation returned.

Crawling out from behind the boulder, he crept closer to his campsite until he reached his bed. Feeling about, he found a neat, round hole clear through the thick blanket and the oilskin. Dang it. That wasn't going to be watertight anymore. He lay down, realizing that his heart was pounding in his ears.

Then it registered. Someone had tried to kill him. Shoot him in his sleep, no less.

Zeke lay awake for the rest of the night. He didn't even dare whistle for Hoedown, even though he couldn't hear the horse moving nearby. At dawn, he carefully raised his head, looked about, and then peeked over the boulder. There was a disturbance on the rock surface, but more telling than that, there were a few drops of blood.

A twig snapped behind him. Zeke whirled around, both hands reaching for his LeMats. Hoedown nickered as he stepped through the brush, his snapped hobbles trailing from one hoof.

"You crazy horse," Zeke said, relief rushing through him.

There wasn't time for breakfast. He had to find his mother fast. If people were so desperate to kill him, the trail must be hot. As he saddled up, Zeke's mind wandered back to his conversation with the barkeep at the saloon. It dawned on him that the man had very specifically mentioned that he wouldn't want to work for Mr. Bennet. He hadn't said specifically why, though, and that piqued Zeke's interest.

"I reckon that Bennet ranch is the most likely place to start," Zeke said softly to Hoedown. He walked the horse for a while, taking a wide, roundabout route. If anyone was following him, he wanted them to think he was leaving Booneville, but not in a hurry. At first, he headed directly east, watching his back trail every now and then when he had cover and the lay of the land allowed it.

At noon, satisfied that nobody was following him, he found

a shady place to rest, built a fire, and brewed some coffee. After digging around in his saddlebags, he found a forgotten hunk of hardtack and soaked it in the coffee. It wasn't much, but it was better than nothing. For a while, he slept, but the sun was only halfway down the western sky when he woke, anxious to continue his search.

Approaching the back-to-back B Ranch from the north, Zeke found himself at the rear of the ranch house. It had an impressive vegetable garden, rows of pumpkin plants and melon plants, a corn patch, cabbages, carrots, beanstalks, just about anything a fellow could grow out there. A woman was moving among the rows with a large basket on her hip.

Zeke moved in closer. He waited until she was at the edge of the garden, with the tallest corn plants hiding them both from sight of the ranch house. Then he stepped out from behind the boulder that had hidden him from her sight.

"If you're Lizzie Sullivan, ma'am, I got to talk to you," he said, keeping his voice low. Just loud enough for her to hear.

The woman went deathly white, dropped her basket, and clapped both hands over her mouth, strangling a scream. Her knees didn't seem able to hold her up, and she sank to the ground, her eyes wide and staring. "Are... are you a ghost?" she said, her voice shaking.

"No, ma'am, I'm as real as you are." Zeke stepped forward and held out both hands.

She took them, her own hands shaking like cottonwood leaves in a mountain breeze. "You look like... Wally. But... you can't be. You're too young." Tears spilled over onto her cheeks while her eyes combed his features, looking for what, only she knew.

"I ain't Wally. I'm Zeke." Zeke reached into his pocket and took out the bracelet. He held it out to her, the same way he'd held it out to Walks With Bears. The look on her face left no doubt in Zeke's mind that she recognized it. As she took the trinket and stared at it, her eyes filled with a mixture of tenderness and anguish.

So, he had found her. At last. And now he was about to find the truth, too.

At least, he hoped so.

CHAPTER 7

ENCOUNTER

Lizzie stared at the little strip of silver with her name engraved on it. In her mind's eye, she could see herself fastening it onto the tiny wrist of her son.

"Hotohkôhma'aestse," she said softly, her voice breaking along with her heart.

"I got questions," the young man's voice broke in on her memory. "There somewhere we can talk where no one'll bother us?"

His eyes were dark, like Wally's. Dark and calm, as if he knew who he was and didn't need anyone's permission to be that person. But there were questions in them, too. She could imagine why. In a flood, the memories washed through her mind, and she blinked back the tears.

"Right here is good," she said. "What do you want to know?" She could tell him everything, from the beginning to the present day. Every incident was imprinted indelibly on her memory. But let him first have his questions answered, as well as she could answer them.

Zeke, as he had called himself, simply stared at her for a few moments. He seemed to be trying to figure out which questions

59

he wanted answered first. Then a muscle twitched in his jaw. When he spoke, his tone was brittle.

"Why'd you desert my father? And why didn't you leave me with him if you weren't fixin' to keep me?" His eyes were hard, accusing. "He became a dog soldier, you know that? I reckon that weren't the right way to handle himself, but I also reckon he can't carry the blame all himself. A man's liable to do crazy things when he's betrayed by his woman like that."

Lizzie gasped. She had hardly heard a word after Zeke's first two questions. "Leave you with your father?" she echoed.

"Yeah. Least I would've had family that way."

Lizzie's heart was pounding in her throat. "You mean he's still alive?" she whispered.

"Sure, he's alive." Zeke looked confused. Then a look of realization dawned in his eyes. "You didn't know that did you?"

Lizzie shook her head. "I thought he was... dead. I thought you were dead." Then she ran out of words.

Zeke's features had softened, and yet there was still that steely look in his eye. He was after truth, it was clear. And he wasn't going to just believe anything he heard. "Your pa tried to kill my pa; you know?"

Lizzie shook her head, though she didn't feel as much shock as most people might, hearing that said about their father. "I didn't know. He told me the army had killed Wally. He told me your father had stolen you and that you'd both been killed when the army chased him down."

She wished she hadn't believed those lies, but her father had sounded so triumphant, his elation so genuine, she had felt sure it was so.

"My pa never stole me. I grew up with a family of emigrants who sold me to the Nez Percé as a slave. Reckon I was a slave for those emigrants, too, when I think about it. I just didn't know it, being little as I was." Her son's voice was bitter but also reflective.

A short silence passed as both mother and son processed what they had just learned.

Eventually, Zeke broke the silence. "I reckon we've all been lied to. Pa thinks you left him on purpose. Went back to your own people."

"How could he think that?" Lizzie asked, aghast.

"Because you never came back. Leastways, that's what I figured from what he said. But maybe your pa lied to him, too. Wouldn't be too much of a stretch, considerin' he tried to beef him. Last I checked, lyin's a heck of a lot easier than killin' a man."

That was true.

The shock was gradually starting to wear off, and Lizzie took a good look at her son. It was easy to see he was Wally's son, too. And the brown, wavy hair, he must have inherited that from her. It was hard to believe the tiny baby she'd held in her arms in Wally's mother's lodge was this tall, handsome, capable young man. Pride welled up in her heart.

Her son seemed to be readjusting his thoughts and perceptions around her existence. Considering his first two questions had been based on faulty beliefs, he seemed hesitant to ask any more. Perhaps it was time for her to have some questions answered.

"How did you know where to find me?" Lizzie asked.

"Pa told me the last place he knew where you were was Booneville."

A stab of disappointment shot through Lizzie's heart. He'd had an idea where she was, and he hadn't come looking for her? Why not? Zeke likely wouldn't know the answer to her unvoiced question.

"Where is he now?" she asked.

"In Indian Territory, on the reservation," Zeke replied.

Of course. He probably wasn't even allowed to travel beyond those borders. At least not without assimilating into the White man's world, and Lizzie knew he would not do that. She wouldn't have wanted him to anyway.

A sudden sense of hopelessness washed over her. So many wasted years. So much senseless heartache. Tears began to roll down her cheeks without her even aware she was beginning to cry.

"I can't tell you how many nights I sat by my window, imagining myself riding over the hills to your father's village and taking you in my arms again," she said.

Zeke shifted his weight. Then he sat down beside her on the ground.

"Then I'd cry myself to sleep thinking it was useless to dream such things about people who were long dead."

Zeke reached out his hand.

Lizzie took it, trying to shake the feeling she was still dreaming.

"I got to know. If you'd had the teeniest idea we were still suckin' air, would you have come a-huntin' us?"

Lizzie nodded vehemently. "Nothing would have stopped me."

Zeke's eyes told her he believed her. Or at the very least, that he badly wanted to. "It ain't too late, Ma," he said softly. "I can take you there right now."

Ma. Lizzie almost started to her feet and headed for the stables and a horse. Instead, she gripped her son's hand tightly. "No, Zeke. It would mean all our deaths. It's worse now than it was before. My father..." She trailed off.

How to tell her son the horrible predicament she was in? How could she possibly endanger him that way? If he was anything like his father, he wouldn't stand for it, and that would result in chaos. He didn't know his grandfather. Maybe it was better he never did.

Zeke looked distrustful of her sudden hesitation. She had to tell him something.

"You don't understand," she said, praying silently for wisdom. "The man I'm married to, by arrangement of my father, he doesn't even know I have a child. He's likely to kill me if he finds out. Especially if he finds out the father of my child is Cheyenne. I can't go to Wally either. If my father finds out, and he has ways of finding out almost anything, he'll kill us all. We can't risk it."

Now that she had discovered her true husband and her precious son were both alive, the thought of them being snatched from her life a second time terrified her. At all costs, her discovery had to be kept a secret. She only hoped Zeke would understand.

"I told my pa I'd go right back there soon as I find out anything. A week from now, he'll know everything you just told me. I don't know that I'd be able t' stop him comin' to look for ya. And then the sparks'll fly for sure, anyhow."

The temptation was strong, but she couldn't do it. Maybe Wally would understand. Maybe they could figure something out later. She needed time. She couldn't think straight.

"You take a message to your pa," she said, thinking how strange those words felt in her mouth, how ethereal it was to know she was speaking to the son she had thought was dead all these years.

"Tell him I'll find a way to get to him. I don't know how, yet, but I will. Just, please, tell him not to come looking for me. I couldn't bear it if he was killed now that I've found him after all this time. And my father will shoot him on sight. I know that without a doubt. He has too much to lose."

Zeke couldn't possibly understand what her words meant,

but there was no time for explanations now. Zeke had to get away before they were spotted, and questions were asked. It would be almost impossible for her to get away from the Bennet ranch if her father's suspicions were aroused.

"Go, now, Zeke," she said earnestly.

For a moment longer, he sat and stared at her, his eyes troubled. He clearly knew there was more to it than she had told him. Her son was no fool. She had to trust that he would trust her. "All right," he said at last. "I'll tell my pa what you said. After that, it's his row to hoe."

That was as much as she could hope for in the moment.

"Good. Now, go. Before someone sees you and starts asking questions. My husband, Mr. Bennet, is ridiculously jealous."

Zeke nodded and stood to his feet. He stood looking at her a moment longer, as if he wanted to imprint her image on his memory. Then he turned away.

"Zeke, wait," Lizzie said.

He stopped and turned back to face her.

"Did your pa tell you your name?"

Zeke shook his head.

"After you were born, the first thing I saw was the evening star in a red glowing sky. Your father and I named you Hotohkôhma'aestse. It means Red Star."

A moment of silence passed. Then Zeke gave her a sad smile. "I like it," he said.

Before Lizzie could respond, he disappeared into the brush growing on the hillside. For a moment, Lizzie stared at the space where her own flesh and blood had just stood, her mind and heart in turmoil. Then she retrieved her dropped basket and went back to breaking off young corn for supper. Her heart was pounding. She wondered how she'd be able to keep the smile off her face. Or the frown, for that matter.

She'd have to try her best. Blake couldn't be alerted to the fact that anything had changed. That anything had made her happy. Or angry. Perhaps it would help not to think of what her father had done. Something far worse than what he'd told her. And yet, despite the horrible things they had all been through because of her father's selfish actions, those actions also meant there was a chance she could see Wally again.

Her heart leaped at the thought then immediately shrank back. It would only put them both in danger. If Zeke was right, if her father really had tried to kill Wally, he would surely be only too willing to finish the job now. And yet she couldn't help wondering what it would be like to see him face to face once more. If she could only have a few hours with him.

Back in the house, Lizzie paused in front of the long mirror in the hall, wondering what Wally would see when—if—he saw her again. She hadn't changed all that much in twenty years, except that there were more lines on her face and the lighter streaks in her hair glinted with silver as much as with gold.

And her eyes were wiser. That was different. The starry dreaminess in them was gone, replaced with slightly jaded skepticism. And an edge of rebellion she hadn't noticed before.

What if she did go with Zeke? Today. No. That would be suicide, wouldn't it?

ZEKE FOUND Hoedown still browsing on sagebrush under the overhang he'd left the horse in. He mounted up and rode along from tree clump to tree clump, careful not to move too fast. Quick movements tended to attract more attention than slow ones.

He tried in vain to keep his thoughts quiet. The news he had just heard changed almost everything he had believed, perhaps feared, to be true about his parents. Everything was different now that he knew his mother had never wanted to abandon him, nor his father. They were all victims. Cruelly kept apart by the one man who should have protected them all. United by a common enemy, even though they were miles apart.

He couldn't shake the image of his mother's haunted eyes. It was strange how he hadn't thought of what she might have been through until he met her. Until he saw her face to face and heard her story. Surely, he could have guessed that it was possible she might be innocent?

He'd always thought of himself as being a fair-minded fellow, ready to give anyone the benefit of the doubt, but he had assumed his own mother's guilt before giving her a chance to say her piece. He would let it be a lesson. But what would his father's reaction be to the message from his mother? Would he believe it? And if he did, would Zeke be able to stop him going to look for his long-lost bride?

It was a risk he had to take, and there was no time to waste. His father was a whole week's ride away, unless he traveled at night. Then he could make up two or three days, though he would be exhausted at the end of a ride like that. And so would Hoedown. After twenty years of waiting, though, it felt wrong to make Walks With Bears wait a day longer than he needed to.

But first, he would have to stock up on provisions. Most likely, town would be quiet that time of day, and he wasn't sure he'd be able to stock up anywhere else.

His mind made up, Zeke pointed Hoedown's head toward Booneville and headed for the trail. Just as the horse's hooves hit the sandy wagon track, a voice hailed him.

"Hey! Hey, you! Ain't you the half-breed I raced up in Fountain?"

Zeke didn't even look around. He knew what he'd see, and he wasn't about to get an eyeful before he absolutely had to.

"Hey! I'm talkin' to you!"

Zeke reined in Hoedown, but he did not turn around. Instead, he sat casually in the saddle, his eyes trained stoically on the track ahead.

"I'd know that dang horse anywhere," the man said, coming past Hoedown and swinging his horse around so that he blocked the way forward. "Never figured I'd run into you in my own backyard." The man looked smug. Zeke looked past him and kept his expression bland. "Don't got your White mama and papa to fight your battles for you now, eh? Let's see how you hold up when it's just you and me."

"I ain't on the prod, mister. I got places to be, so if it's all the same to you, we can do this some other time." Zeke kept looking past his tormentor.

"If it's all the same to me, eh? Well, it ain't all the same to me." The man reached for his pistol; one lip curled back in a hate-filled snarl. "I said I want to fight you. Now. So, you'll climb down and fight me, or I'll empty that saddle for you."

This time Zeke looked into the man's eyes. He'd seen, during his years running with Hezekiah Lightfoot's gang and other outlaws, you could usually tell when a fellow was going to shoot, just by looking into his eyes. Especially a blustering fellow like this one.

Zeke kept his hands free of the brace of LeMats buckled around his hips and held the man's gaze. No need to give the crazy White man any excuses.

CHAPTER 8

ESCAPE

"Well, hello, Larry. I see you've met Zeke."

Lizzie's voice fell on Zeke's ears and made his stomach twist into a tight, fearful knot. The man who had been just about to shoot Zeke, or fight him, or both, went a little white in the face and quickly holstered his pistol.

"Howdy do, Miz Bennet," he said. "I had no idea you knew this feller."

"I wouldn't expect you to, Larry," Lizzie said as her horse drew alongside Zeke's. "He's a new ranch hand who's just joined us. I was hoping I'd catch up with him since I needed someone to ride to town with me. Mr. Bennet is just too busy right now and there are some things I'd like to fetch."

She turned her head to look at Zeke, her face veiled with calm indifference. "Would you be so kind as to let me ride with you, Zeke? My husband would never let me ride anywhere alone. It's just not safe."

"I'd be honored, ma'am," Zeke said, falling in with her ploy and hoping Larry would fall for it.

"Well, I'll be danged. Small world, ain't it," Larry said. His eyes darted from one to the other, as if he was trying to catch them communicating secretly, but he nudged his horse out of their way and doffed his hat to his employer's wife. "I got some work on the ranch, myself, otherwise I might have ridden along, too."

"As you wish," Lizzie said with a perfect poker face. "I'm sure one guardian is enough for me, though. Nobody in their right mind would even think of molesting the wife of Blake Bennet."

Larry glanced at the LeMats in Zeke's gun belt. "I sure hope you know how t' use those things," he said, narrowing his eyes. Then he clapped his heels to his horse's sides and headed toward the ranch in a cloud of dust.

Lizzie tossed her chin toward town and put her own heels to her horse's sides. Zeke followed along as his mother led off at a fast trot.

"You sure arrived in the nick of time, and I won't say I'm not grateful," Zeke said as Hoedown matched pace with his mother's liver chestnut stallion. "But I'm wonderin' why you came after me."

"I'm riding back with you. Back to Wally," Lizzie said, her eyes scanning the surrounding hillsides, her tone firm and decisive.

Zeke almost reined Hoedown to a dead stop. "But that's crazy, Ma! You said yourself Bennet and your pa would finish one or all of us off if you did that."

"I know what I said. Can't a woman change her mind?"

Zeke didn't know what to say to that. She had said she was going to find a way. Maybe she had, though it seemed a mighty short time to figure out anything foolproof.

"To tell you the truth, Zeke, I don't care what Bennet, or my father does." Her words cut through the air like knives. "Your grandfather forced me to marry that brute, and when it became clear there weren't going to be any heirs born for him, he said it was my fault. My father swore he'd kill me if I dared let on I knew it wasn't my womb that was barren."

She stopped speaking suddenly and slowed her horse. Zeke reined Hoedown back. The horse tossed his head impatiently. Zeke knew how he felt.

"I'm sorry. I shouldn't be telling you all this. I just…"

"You can tell me anything you like, Ma. I've seen things that'll turn your blood to ice."

She held his gaze for a few moments. "You sure I can tell you anything?"

"Anything," Zeke assured her. He'd had his fill of secrets for a lifetime.

"Bennet beats me. But my father won't believe it when I tell him. He never hits hard enough to bruise, at least not badly. It's always just one or two. He chokes me, too, when he's mad enough. The thing is, though, he manages to control himself just enough not to cause bruising. He scares me, Zeke, but I've had as much as I can take."

Zeke felt as if someone had stuck a red-hot fire poker right through his stomach. His ears began to burn, his heart pounded against his ribs. "I swear, if I ever lay eyes on the yellow-bellied snake, I'll drill him through with every last bit of lead in these LeMats of mine!"

Lizzie shook her head, her eyes misty with tears. "You see? I shouldn't have told you. Don't waste your anger on people who don't care about anything other than themselves. They're not worth the trouble."

Zeke slowed Hoedown to a walk. "You sure we should go into town together? I was aiming to get some provisions for the trail, but…" Zeke trailed off. Things had just gotten almighty complicated. Now there were reasons neither of them should be seen in town, as a matter of fact.

Lizzie didn't seem fazed. "Ride with me till I tell you to strike out. Then go east. You'll find an old Cheyenne trail running dead south. When it hits the river, take cover and wait for me. I'll get what we need."

"How do you know what to get—" Zeke began.

"I am the wife of Walks With Bears. I know what's needed for a week on the trail." Lizzie grinned and nudged her horse into a spanking trot again.

Zeke smiled and touched his heels to Hoedown's sides, giving the horse permission to catch up. It made perfect sense why his father would have chosen a bride like Elizabeth Sullivan. A man like Walks With Bears needed a woman with spunk. And Zeke himself? He'd dreamed of how his mother must have been, and Lizzie fitted his imaginings to a T.

When Lizzie showed Zeke where to turn off, he obeyed immediately. No more questioning. It was clear she knew what she was about. He found the trail and followed it down to the river, turning off into the brush when the riverbank was still a way off. Riding up behind a small outcrop just big enough to hide behind and watch the trail, he dismounted and waited.

It wasn't long after that he spotted his mother riding to join him. She was right smart about it, too, watching her back trail and staying on the hard-packed, trodden-down part of the trail where her horse's hooves would leave little or no sign, especially where leaves and dead grass lay scattered across it.

"We'll have to push on a bit if we're aiming to get a head start before nightfall," Zeke said when he joined her.

"I was thinking of that," Lizzie said, casting a worried glance at the sun hastening westward. "If you think we should travel at night, don't hold back on my account. I'll do what it takes, Zeke, I swear it."

"Let's go," Zeke said with a smile. There was no doubt in his mind that all hell would break loose once Blake Bennet figured out Lizzie wasn't coming home. And then there was the issue of the Larry fellow. Of course, he might even already have told a few listening ears what he had seen on the road to town. More specifically, who he had seen. The clock was ticking.

They didn't talk much while they rode. That suited Zeke fine. He was still adjusting his thoughts to the truth he had learned that day. Only yesterday he'd been ready to ride back and tell his father there wasn't anything to be done about his heartache, and now, here he was, bringing Walks With Bears the best news either of them could have imagined possible. In the flesh. Literally.

Zeke and Lizzie rode far into the night, covering their tracks when and wherever the opportunity presented itself. Both had been well trained by the Native inhabitants of the land. Zeke felt a kinship growing between them, a unity of purpose, of understanding. More than once, they laughed when Lizzie finished Zeke's sentences for him while he explained how they could conceal the signs of their passing.

When the Big Dipper had rotated almost all the way around the North Star, Zeke called a halt. He had been watching for secure resting places on his way to Booneville, and now he led his mother to one of the places he had spotted and earmarked in his mind. Quickly and quietly, Lizzie set about making a small fire to cook some of the bacon and beans she'd bought in town. Zeke went out and did a little scouting.

When he got back, the food was cooked and smelled amazing. He wolfed it down, suddenly conscious he hadn't eaten since he'd almost choked on that ancient piece of hardtack he'd soaked in his coffee. It hit him with a jolt that it was more than twelve hours ago.

"You said you lived with the Nez Percé for a while," Lizzie said, watching him eat. She was only nibbling on her food, clearly not as ravenous as he was.

"Yeah." Zeke swallowed a mouthful of bacon, beans, and biscuit. "The emigrants sold me to 'em when I was around seven. Lived with 'em for about three years or so. Then they were drygulched by a posse of emigrants takin' revenge for a raid. I was down by the river. Heard the shootin' and screamin' and trailed the fellers who did it. They figured they were the heroes of the hour. Trouble is, I knew for a fact our people, the Nez Percé, didn't do no raidin' of wagons or emigrants, even though White men were takin' over all our lands, lookin' for yellow iron."

"Gold," Lizzie said, shaking her head sadly. "It'll be the curse of this land for generations to come. You mind my words."

"Gold ain't the problem," Zeke corrected his mother. "Gold's been lyin' peaceful-like, in the ground, mindin' its own business for hundreds of years. It's greedy folks who think gold will make 'em better than other folks. They're the curse. The folks who'll just as soon shoot ya as look at ya, all for the sake of gettin' to the gold before ya."

Lizzie looked at him as if she were seeing him for the first time. "Yes, I do believe you're right," she said slowly. "'The love of money is the root of all evil,' so the Holy Scriptures say. It stands to reason that one could replace 'money' with 'gold.'"

"We should get some shut-eye," Zeke said, scratching around in the burned stumps and ashes of the fire so that the flames died down and only glowing embers remained. "There's only a couple hours before daybreak, and we'll want to move out before the sun's up."

Lizzie lay down and wrapped herself in the bedroll she'd brought along. "Good night, son," she said softly. She said it a lot like the way Jessie used to say it. But it meant a whole lot more.

"G'night, Ma," Zeke replied as he rolled himself up in his own bedroll. It felt good to call someone that, knowing she really was his flesh and blood. He was finally beginning to find out where he came from, who he belonged to. Where his place was.

Tanner and Jessie had taught him what it meant to be loved and part of a family, but they weren't his kin, and there was just something different about knowing your blood kin. Something he couldn't describe in mere words.

Perhaps the closest he could get was to say that, even though he and his parents might not always be together, and Zeke might one day have his own family and his own home, he would always know where he belonged. Although, that where wasn't a physical place. It was a place in the heart, the soul. A place in the spirit.

"Did your pa tell you how he and I met?" Lizzie's voice reached Zeke through the darkness.

"He sure did," Zeke said. "Told me how your pa chased him off the ranch, even though he brought a bride price of ten ponies. That's the bride price of a chief's daughter."

"I know," Lizzie said softly. She was quiet for a little while, and when she spoke again, her voice was deeply sad. "You need to know something, Zeke. I know I've told you a lot of awful things your grandfather did, but he's not just a bad man."

Zeke didn't reply. He wasn't sure he even wanted to think about it. Trying to see good in someone who had done the things Sullivan had done was hard enough. Knowing that person was your grandfather was a horrible, nauseating thought.

"He's bitter and twisted all out of shape, but that's because he's a deeply wounded man. His father and two brothers were killed by Seminoles in Georgia when the army tried to forcibly remove the tribe from their ancestral lands. He grew up with a stepfather who beat him and married young. He and my mother decided to move to Missouri. She had family there, and he wanted to get away from his stepfather."

Zeke listened quietly in the darkness. He didn't want to feel sorry for a man who had openly threatened his mother's life. Still, he couldn't help empathizing a little.

"After a few years and three children, my parents decided to move down to New Mexico Territory. Folks said there was plenty of land available and even talk of gold, though the gold rush was long over, by more than a decade. So, they hit the Santa Fe trail. When they were a week out of Dodge City, my pa took me for a ride with a handful of other men in the wagon train when they went to scout. When they got back, the wagons had been burned, oxen slaughtered, horses stolen, and not a soul survived."

"I reckon my grandpa hates all Indians, don't he, Ma?" Zeke said dryly.

"Yes. He does. And he thinks he has good reason."

"Guess I can't fault him for that." Zeke still didn't know what to make of what he was learning.

Knowing your own grandfather hated you didn't make much more sense when you knew he simply hated the nation you represented. Wars and tribal hatred were common between the first peoples of the land, and yet somehow, surely, the fact that he also had some of Sullivan's blood pulsing through his veins, surely that must make some kind of difference?

"Actually, you can fault him for that," Lizzie said, as if reading Zeke's mind. "You are not the man who set those wagons alight and killed my mother and sisters. Your father is not the man who killed Theodore Sullivan's father and brothers. Men in every nation on earth are capable of evil and capable of good. The color of a man's skin does not make him evil any more than it makes him good. It is what is inside his heart, what drives the choices he makes, that determines a man's character."

Zeke listened to his mother's voice. It was firm and emphatic, filled with an aching melancholy as much as with unsentimental wisdom. He lay awake for a while after that. Not because he wasn't tired, but because his head was still spinning with everything that had transpired in the few short days since he had found his father and now his mother.

At last, he managed to drift off into a light sleep but woke early with the first few twitters of the dawn chorus. Lizzie was sleeping peacefully. How she managed it, he didn't know. Perhaps it was simply pure exhaustion.

The next two days were uneventful, except for the fact they shared more about their lives, their dreams, their regrets, and the lessons they'd learned. By the third day, mother and son were steadily nearing the reservation where Walks With Bears was waiting. Lizzie grew quieter, as if she could sense they were getting close. Zeke left her to her thoughts. He couldn't imagine what it must feel like to be in her shoes.

He blamed himself for what happened next. His thoughts were wandering, his focus too much inward and not enough on what was going on around him. He was thinking of his mother, his father, the past, and the way forward.

The land was flat, not a tree in sight, no place to hide. He should have seen their dust cloud a long way off. He should have kept their own dust cloud down to a minimum. As it was, he first heard the hoof beats behind them when the riders were already almost upon them. Twisting round in his saddle, he saw the row of five horses gaining on them.

His stomach sank into his boots as he turned back to face Lizzie. "I reckon your pa missed you," he said dryly.

Lizzie nodded, her lips in a tight line. "We keep riding. Don't stop. If he has anything to say, he can say it on the move."

"Whatever you say, Ma," Zeke said. "I'll back you up, whatever you think we got to do." This was her battle. He knew that. He didn't have any say in how to fight it, but he hoped she knew that he would follow her lead and have her back every inch of the way. He deliberately slowed Hoedown so that he was slightly behind Lizzie's horse.

"Lizzie! Stop right there!" a coarse male voice cried out. "You've got some explaining to do, young lady!"

CHAPTER 9

DECEPTION

Lizzie calmly kept on riding as if nobody had spoken. She didn't look around; she didn't slow her pace or increase it even by a smidgen.

"Blast it, Lizzie! I said stop!"

Lizzie continued to ignore the voice behind them. She kept her eyes facing forward, her head up, her back ramrod straight, her shoulders pushed back.

Zeke followed her example, knowing in that moment that he would carry that image of his mother in his heart for the rest of his days.

"By thunder, you obstinate child! I swear I'm ready to throttle all the rebellion out of you!"

The hoof beats increased in tempo, and Zeke watched out of the corner of his eye as the posse trotted past them at a smart pace. There was an old man who he guessed must be his grandfather, a younger man who looked a lot like Lizzie, two more men Zeke had seen around the ranch during his scouting expeditions, and his old friend Larry.

They crossed in front of Lizzie's horse and drew rein, clearly intent on blocking the way.

"I'm riding through, Father," Lizzie said in clear, calm tones. "Whatever you have to say to me, I'll listen to, but I'm not stopping or slowing down."

"Will you be sensible, woman? Go home to your husband and quit fooling around with this savage!"

Lizzie's horse had reached the posse by that point, and he tossed his head and squealed. The other horses jostled each other, trying to dodge the liver chestnut's teeth at the end of his snaking neck. Neither their rider's spurs nor the reins slapped against their shoulders could make them stay put.

Lizzie spurred her horse on, holding her father's gaze as she pushed between him and his posse. "You don't understand, Father. I *am* going home to my husband. The man you forced upon me was never my husband. I was already spoken for. My son is taking me to see my real husband, and I won't let you or anyone else get in my way," Lizzie said as her horse passed through the posse and kept going.

Zeke kept Hoedown close on the haunches of his mother's horse. The Appaloosa was feeling the tension in the air too, throwing a nip or two at the posse horses as he passed through. At that moment, he looked up into the face of his grandfather.

Although the man's face was wrinkled and sun browned, his blue eyes blazed with vigor and fire. He was tall and lanky, and spry as a man probably half his age. He sat on his horse with a bold and confident ease, but his hands were quick and ready, his eyes alert and watchful.

As he caught Zeke's gaze, a look of shock crossed his face. "Your son?" he snapped, breaking eye contact with Zeke and turning his horse so that he kept pace with Lizzie.

"Yes, Father, my son. The one you sold to emigrants like a common slave. Did you know they sold him to the Nez Percé? Your own flesh and blood you sell into slavery. How do you expect me to love or respect a man who does a thing like that? A man who lied and said my husband and my son were dead."

"Pa?" the young man, who looked like Lizzie, spoke up at Zeke's other shoulder. "Is that true?"

"Not now, Yule! That's not important. We're here to get your sister back home."

Yule didn't reply. Zeke looked around at the others, wondering why they weren't forcing Lizzie to stop. Larry glared at him, the lust for revenge still glittering in his eyes.

"I'm warning you, Lizzie, if you don't come back home, I'll make life unbearable for you."

"It already was unbearable, Father," came the flat reply. "Now, you can either escort me to meet with my true husband and tell him the truth firsthand of what you did, or you can leave me be and tell Blake Bennet that his nuptials were never legal to begin with. At least he still has time to find another heifer to produce his all-important offspring."

"All right," Sullivan said hotly. "I'll go tell Bennet your position and let him discipline you in his own way." He spun his horse around and began riding in the opposite direction. Larry looked confused. Yule looked relieved, and a little torn. He gave Lizzie a sympathetic glance before following behind his father. The two other men wheeled their horses around, looking bored.

Zeke couldn't help wondering what Sullivan was up to. Lizzie had said she was sure he would kill her if he found out where she was headed. And yet, here he was, giving up so easily. Why hadn't he brought Bennet along in the first place? Unless he had hoped to get Lizzie back without Bennet knowing the true circumstances of her disappearance.

Whatever the case, Zeke felt uneasy. A man like Sullivan wasn't to be trusted. He had a reputation and a lot of money riding on his daughter's obedience. That much had become clear to Zeke after his conversations with his mother. He only wished he knew what Sullivan was up to.

YULE FOLLOWED along behind his father, trying to reconcile what he had just heard with what he had believed his whole life. The man Lizzie had referred to as her son was clearly a half-breed. His swarthy facial features, his almost black, piercing, yet calm eyes, his lean, muscular build. The man's cowboy garb didn't do much to hide the fact of his parentage.

But Lizzie married? To an Indian? He couldn't imagine that. And yet his father hadn't disputed that fact. Then again, Sullivan never disputed anything. He simply stated what he believed to be true and left the squabbling to the magpies of society, as he was fond of saying.

Yule rode up alongside Sullivan. "Father, what's going on?"

Sullivan gave him an icy, piercing glare. "Your sister is acting like a child. And we're going to teach her a lesson," he said bitterly.

"Was she really married to an Indian?" Yule couldn't help asking.

Sullivan merely gave him a baleful glare and went on riding.

Yule was left to puzzle over the conundrum himself. His mother had died soon after he was born, and Lizzie had cared for him like a mother. When he was only five years old, Lizzie was kidnapped by Indians, or so he had been told.

She had been rescued a bit more than a year later and returned with a baby boy, but the baby's father had tried to steal him, and they had both been killed.

Yule slowed his horse absentmindedly. Again, that was what he had been told. But that apparently wasn't true, if Lizzie was to be believed. And Yule was leaning toward believing her.

He couldn't imagine his half-sister going to such extreme lengths to ride all the way to Indian Territory to find a man who was dead. And she had called the half-breed her son. Lizzie might be headstrong, but she wasn't beef headed.

"Yule! Don't lag behind!" his father's sharp rebuke jolted him from his pondering.

When Yule caught up to the rest of the men, his father looked back and then reined in his horse.

"We're not going back to Bennet just yet," he said, glancing at all the men in turn. "We're going to follow them." He jerked his head back in the direction they had just come from.

"We know they're headed for Indian Territory, we just don't know where. We'll have to get Lizzie back before she reaches that blasted village, or we'll have more than just her son to contend with."

"Get her back?" Yule echoed. Lizzie hadn't been kidnapped this time, either. That was abundantly clear. Yule couldn't help it, but he was beginning to see his father in a very different light.

He had always thought of Sullivan as strong and self-contained. A gentleman and a proud one, at that, albeit a pretty hard taskmaster. But Yule had always believed it was just lazy ranch hands who thought of Sullivan as merciless and cruel.

"Yes, get her back," Sullivan snapped irritably. "And you're going to do it. She trusts you the most of all of us. Make her think you want to know more about what happened, and when her guard is down—and the half-breed's—you take her and do whatever you have to with him."

"But, Father, what if he fights me? He looks stronger than—"

"Shoot him," Sullivan said flatly. "It's time you learned to defend yourself."

Yule's stomach twisted into a worried knot. He had always

obeyed his father. Perhaps that was why he'd never felt the infamous Sullivan fury poured down upon his head. He didn't want to obey now, but something told him he had better go along with the plan. He wasn't all that keen to find out whether the rumors about his father's cruelty were true.

"All right, Father. When do you want me to do it?"

"That's a good lad," Sullivan said. "Tonight. If the half-breed survives, he'll have a hard time following us in the dark."

"Yes, Father."

YULE RODE CLOSER to the dark bulks of two horses tethered out on the flat in the gloom of dusk. Simply riding those few miles out to his sister's camp, away from his father and the others, had been fairly nerve wracking.

Despite the fact everybody knew the Indians were mostly all safely ordered onto their reservations, there were still those militant bands of resistors who roamed the prairie, like Quanah Parker and his band of Comanche. Yule hoped he wouldn't lose his life before he got to his sister and then safely back to his father's posse.

"Hello, the camp!" he called out as he neared the place from where the aroma of fried bacon and refried beans wafted on the air.

"Who's there?" a male voice asked in clipped syllables.

"It's Yule. I'm here to see Lizzie. I'm alone."

"Yule?" Lizzie's voice came out of the darkness. "Did Father send you?"

"Yeah, he did. But before I do anything, I want some questions answered. I know you'll tell me the truth. You always have." He could see her vaguely in the fading light of evening as she stepped closer and took his hand. He'd never had a mother.

Lizzie was the closest thing to maternal care and affection that he had ever known.

"Sit down," Lizzie said.

Yule obeyed.

"Now fire away and I'll try to answer everything you need to know," Lizzie said, her voice sad but with a tinge of humor.

"Pa said you were kidnapped when I was five. Is that true?"

"No. I chose to go to the Cheyenne village to live with Wally. We loved each other, and I loved—I still love—the ways of his people."

"So you married a Cheyenne fellow?" Yule wanted to be sure there was no mistake.

"I did. In a special ceremony with as much meaning as any you'll find in any Christian church."

"And this fellow here is your son from that marriage?"

"He is. His name is Zeke." She hesitated. "That's what he calls himself, at least. Zeke, this is my half-brother, Yule. Remember I told you my father married again, but his wife died soon after childbirth?"

The young half-breed man stepped forward and held out his hand. "Pleasure to make your acquaintance, Yule," Zeke said, sounding like any cowhand on the Bennet ranch.

Yule pumped the man's arm, noticing that his handshake was firm, the kind a fellow could trust. "I never figured I'd find out I have more kin today, but life sure is full of surprises, isn't it?" Yule said, releasing his newfound nephew's hand and running his own hand through his hair.

Lizzie laughed. "I never figured I'd be riding out to see Wally. Never in my wildest dreams..." Her voice choked up, and she trailed off.

In that moment, Yule knew there was no way he could honor his father's request. "Pa sent me to kidnap you and take you back, Lizzie," he said bluntly. "But I'm of no such mind. If I were you two, I'd hightail it out of here, as the cowhands say. I'll tell Father that Zeke overpowered me and you headed off in some other direction."

Lizzie gripped her half-brother's wrist. "If he finds out you lied, he'll make sure you suffer, Yule. He might disown you."

"Then let him," Yule said. "I always trusted Father. Thought I wanted to be like him someday. Thought he was a big hero for rescuing my sister from a wild, crazy Indian. Now I find out it was all a lie. How's a fellow supposed to trust his father after that? I can't help wondering what else he's lying to me about."

Lizzie hugged him impulsively. "I'll never forget this, Yule," she said. "If you ever need any help, you come looking for me and Wally and Zeke. We're your family. Always remember that."

Yule's throat felt thick and his eyes watery. He'd never cried about anything in his life, following his father's stoic example, but this was something different from anything he'd ever experienced. A sudden thought struck him. "Why didn't you tell me the truth before, Lizzie?"

His sister pulled back, her hands resting on his shoulders. "The less you knew, the better, Yule. I didn't want to drag you into the whole sordid affair. As long as you didn't know anything, you were safe."

"You're some kind of woman, sis," Yule said, the stinging sensation in his eyes intensifying. "Now, get moving. You'll need a good head start. And cover your tracks. One of the cowhands father brought along is a seasoned tracker."

"How about we make it look like a grand old scuffle happened here?" Zeke suggested out of the blue.

Yule paused, weighing the proposition in his mind. It would be a good thing to be able to back up his story with some physical signs of a struggle.

"And make sure you follow us as far as the Canadian River. We'll go upstream a ways and double back south of the river."

Yule nodded. The three took hands and did some violent kicking and stomping on the ground, making sure they made a big disturbance. Then Yule rolled in the dirt and made sure his clothes got torn a bit and his skin scratched.

"Now we ride. Fast as we can," Zeke said.

They mounted up, moving as quickly as they could through the darkness, Yule trailing his sister and nephew by a few yards. They reached the river and let their horses walk into the shallows. Yule pulled up alongside Zeke. He held out his hand. By now, the moon had risen and they could see each other better in the silvery light.

"My father isn't worthy of a grandson like you," he said. "I know you'll take good care of Lizzie for me." He turned to face his sister, his throat feeling thick again. "I'd sure love to come visit sometime, sis. The man who wins your heart and fathers a son like Zeke... Well, he's a man I'd be happy to get acquainted with."

"You better come visit, Yule. Or I'll come fetch you myself," Lizzie said.

Zeke turned his horse and began walking the nimble Appaloosa up the river, against the current. Lizzie briefly gripped her half-brother's hand and then followed her son. Yule sat his horse silently in the river, watching them go until he couldn't see any movement in the moonlight anymore.

Then he rode around in the river a while, down the bank and up the bank on both sides. He needed to leave the kinds of tracks that would support the story he was about to tell his father. All the while, a heavy weight of sadness and regret pressed on his chest. The father he had trusted, looked up to, feared, and revered, had lied to him. Lied point-blank and hurt his sister. How could he have been so blind? Everything he had believed to be true was now brought into question.

It was one thing to lead his father and his posse on a wild

goose chase to protect Lizzie and her son, but how was he going to live the rest of his life? Even if his father didn't disown him, how could he continue to live a lie, now that he knew it for what it was?

By the time he got back to Sullivan's camp, Yule was angry and distressed enough that it was laughably easy to make the old man believe he was upset at having been beaten by a half-breed and outwitted by a woman.

"We'll go after them in the morning, Yule," Sullivan said with unnerving confidence. "They won't get far with Larry Quick tracking them. You mark my words."

CHAPTER 10

REUNION

Zeke knew he should be tired, but his head was as clear and alert as it had ever been. He had led his mother up the Canadian river a couple of miles until they found a grassy bank they could ride up onto without leaving much sign. Then he turned Hoedown's head due south, riding until he came to a row of hills. There he turned east, using the stars to guide him, just as the Nez Percé had taught him.

They were making good time. Lizzie was quiet, and he didn't try to make conversation. There would be time enough for that later. They quickly reached the Canadian River once more, where it flowed slightly southward before turning back toward the land of the winter man. When it did that, he would keep his face looking directly east until he reached the place the United States government had designated as Indian Territory.

When they reached that bend, the sky in the east was beginning to turn slate gray. The morning star shone boldly, seeming to call them onward. Without discussing it, they gradually increased their pace as the sun began to glide up out of its bed in the earth.

Zeke kept an eye on their back trail, watching for dust

clouds or the glint of the sun on metal, but he saw nothing. The sun climbed higher and higher into the sky, until it was nearly at its zenith. That was when they crested the rise of a small hill and Zeke saw his father's village in the valley ahead of them.

As they neared the village, his mother slowed her horse and looked at him. "That's the place, isn't it?" she asked, her voice trembling slightly.

"It sure is," Zeke said.

Lizzie nodded. "I'm ready." Her eyes were determined, though she seemed a little paler than Zeke remembered.

He led her down into the village in silence. The women had gone out to the fields to tend to the crops and the cattle. A few old people and small children were seated outside their lodges, the elders preparing the morning meal for their families and the children playing. They looked up as Zeke and Lizzie rode in. One old woman's face lit up when she laid eyes on Lizzie. She came to her feet and raised her hands in the air, shouting something in her native tongue.

Curious heads popped out of wickiups and tipis, stared at Lizzie, and then turned to look in the direction of Walks With Bears's lodge as smiles wreathed their faces.

As they drew near to Walks With Bears's lodge, the flap covering the entrance was thrown aside, and the big man stepped outside, his face full of desperate hope. Zeke heard Lizzie gasp.

"Wally?" she said.

"Lizzie?" He stepped forward, shock written all over his features as he studied her face. "It is true what I hear the old woman shouting?"

"I'm back, Wally." She reined in her horse.

Walks With Bears stepped closer and placed a hesitant hand on the horse's neck.

"If you'll have me," Lizzie added softly.

Walks With Bears looked over at Zeke. "You found her." His voice was filled with disbelief. "So fast."

"Sullivan ain't too happy about it, though, Ného'e. He's likely trying to track us right now." Zeke instinctively knew his father would want the whole truth.

Walks With Bears turned back to look at his wife. Tears were rolling down her cheeks. "I will have you," he said, reaching up and placing his large hands around her waist. He hoisted her out of the saddle onto the ground and folded himself around her.

Zeke looked down and dismounted, not wanting to intrude on his parents' private moment. Only then did he realize the villagers who were present had gathered round, and they began to cheer. Some sang and chanted, others danced in wild, jubilant circles.

The horses snorted and shied as the little crowd closed in on husband and wife, patting them on their backs, shaking their shoulders, howling with undisguised joy, and repeating one word over and over. Zeke recognized it as the name Lizzie had told him the Cheyenne had given her when she became Walks With Bears's wife.

"Mamâhkȩhe'hehe!" they cried. "Curly Woman!"

After a while, the hubbub died down and Rides The Sun sent the happy, still chattering and excited villagers away. Walks With Bears led his wife into his tipi. Zeke and Rides The Sun followed.

There was much to talk about, much to explain. Much to apologize for and much forgiveness to offer. Tears flowed freely from both Lizzie and Walks With Bears. They talked until night fell and their bellies rumbled. Rides The Sun's wife brought food, and they ate and talked some more.

Their words had just begun to run out when the flap of the

tipi was thrown back. Zeke looked up, wondering who would be so rude. His heart nearly stopped when he saw Larry Quick push his way inside. The man's gun was already drawn, his eyes cold and glittering.

"I sure hope you folks don't mind us joinin' the party," he said, stepping aside but pointing the muzzle of his pistol at first one, then another.

Sullivan stepped through the opening behind Larry and let the flap down. His face was rigid, set in a mask of stiff-necked pride. "Lizzie, you're coming back with me, where you belong. Whether you like it or not."

Zeke noticed his grandfather hadn't given anyone else in the lodge even the most cursory glance. They may as well have been invisible, except for the fact that Larry's eyes darted from one to another, daring them to reach for their weapons, of whatever sort they might be.

"I am going nowhere with you, Father," Lizzie said, her voice expressionless. "I already am where I belong."

"Looks like I'll to have to beef that half-breed and his savage father after all, Mister Sullivan," Larry said, looking as if he relished the thought.

Lizzie stepped between Larry and Walks With Bears, who stood to his feet in that moment. Zeke stood up, too, and Larry swung his gun in Zeke's direction. The click of a hammer being drawn back punctuated the tense silence. Zeke got ready to draw, but the look of surprise on Larry's face told him it wasn't Larry who had just armed his weapon.

Larry's eyes flicked back to Lizzie, and Zeke followed his gaze. She stood there, holding what looked like a Navy pocket pistol, and she was pointing it right at Larry.

"You should know, Larry Quick, if my son or my husband dies, so does the man who killed them."

Larry went a sickly shade of gray, and his weapon dropped slightly. But not long enough for Zeke to contemplate shucking a LeMat. Almost at once, Larry lifted his gun again, color flooding his cheeks. "You couldn't shoot a man," he said derisively. "You're a woman."

Lizzie stared at him for a while. Then she seemed to make up her mind about something. "Maybe you're right, Larry," she said, lowering the weapon. "Maybe all that bloodshed isn't necessary."

"Toss me the gun, Miz Bennet," Larry said, looking smug.

"Not so fast. I'll hold onto this until we're far enough away from the village for me to know you won't do anything irresponsible," Lizzie said.

"Ma! What are you doing?" Zeke's voice rang out before he had time to filter his thoughts.

"Trust me, Zeke. It's for the best," Lizzie said, still not taking her eyes off Larry. "Larry, you lead the way. Father, you can follow behind me. But no shooting. I'm coming with you, now, so there's really no reason for you to shoot anybody."

Sullivan chucked his chin in the direction of the tipi entrance. Larry grudgingly pushed the flap open and stepped backward through the opening. Zeke felt as if his heart was being torn out of his chest. He looked at his father. Walks With Bears's face was stoic. Rides The Sun's expression was equally inscrutable.

Frustration gnawed at Zeke's fingers, making them itch to draw a weapon, but he couldn't risk bullets flying around, not after he had worked so hard to find his parents and then bring them back together. Besides, his mother's words rang in his head, *No shooting.*

As soon as Sullivan had stepped out through the entrance behind Lizzie, Zeke darted forward, but his father caught him by the arm.

"Stop, son. That man called Larry; he is tight like a bowstring. He will shoot at shadows. Do not move quickly where he sees."

"But Ného'e! My mother! I can't let them..." He didn't finish his sentence. The sound of the lever action being worked on a rifle stopped him as sure as if it had been fired.

"You the fella who threatened my boy?" Jessie's voice rang out in the night air. "Drop that six-gun of yours right there on the ground, mister, or so help me, I'll shoot your hand off."

"She means it. Trust me," Tanner's mellow tones chimed in. "I'd pay her some mind if I were in your shoes."

Larry cursed in the same moment Zeke sped through the tipi opening, just in time to see the hired gun drop his pistol into the dirt and open his palms for Jessie to see them.

"You sure are a lot smarter than you look," Jessie said. "Now, just to prove that's so, why don't you light a shuck out of here?" For a split second her eye caught Zeke's, and she gave him a wink.

Lizzie darted to Walks With Bears's side.

Sullivan said, "You're just like your mother, Elizabeth. Headstrong and stubborn as a mule. If it wasn't for Bennet, I'd have left you to get yourself killed. As it is, I've tried to give you a way out. We could have made this look like a kidnapping and rescue, but you're leaving me no choice. I'll have to bring Bennet into this and let him sort you out." He walked toward his horse, his back still straight, his head held high and proud.

Lizzie pulled her pocket revolver out again and pointed it at his back. "Why didn't you get rid of me when I was a child, like you got rid of my son? I wouldn't have been any trouble to you then."

Sullivan stopped in his tracks. "Because I loved you," he said softly. "That's why you were with me when the rest of our family and an entire wagon train were murdered by Indian dogs."

"Loved me? Have you ever loved anyone, Father?"

Sullivan turned slowly around. "I loved your mother. She was my whole world, you know? And you, you look just like her. You've got her spirit and her sass, too. When she was killed, I couldn't look at you for days. I hated you, and yet I loved you. I wanted to give you away to a settler family, but I couldn't. You were all I had left of Veronica." He shrugged. "I suppose now both of us have to pay the price for my sentimental blunder."

Zeke glanced between his mother and grandfather. She was still pointing the pistol at her father. He looked like he wanted her to shoot him.

Lizzie began to shake, and tears streamed down her face. "It could have been so different," she said, her voice cracking. Then, all at once, she straightened up. "But this is the way it is, thanks to you, Father." Her voice was stronger now. "The truth is I can't trust you near my family. I'm giving you fair warning. If I ever see you or any of your hired guns anywhere near my family again, I will shoot you myself."

Sullivan didn't move for a moment, simply stood looking at his daughter with a strangely detached look on his face. Then he grunted. "Come on, Larry," he said. He turned away and walked into the darkness, with Larry following behind him.

Zeke stood ready, his hand on his LeMat. Jessie still held her Yellowboy at hip level, the muzzle of the gun following Sullivan and Larry's progress. In the shadows beyond the circle of the firelight, Zeke watched the two men mount up and ride away. Nobody spoke until the sound of thudding hooves and creaking leather faded away into the night.

Then Jessie lowered her rifle, stepped over to Larry's revolver, and picked it up. She dusted it off, checked the load and shoved it into her belt. She straightened up and gave Zeke the biggest grin he'd ever seen on her face.

"Boy am I happy to see the both of you, Ma-Jess," Zeke said, returning her grin. He strode forward and greeted his adoptive parents with a relieved and ecstatic hug. "But I can't help wonderin' how you found us."

Jessie laughed. "After you were gone for three whole weeks, well, I just got plain antsy. Tanner said it was like trying t' keep house with a mama bear whose cub's been stolen. Well, right there, we up and decided to go lookin' for ya. We tried Denver, but folks were mighty tight-lipped up there."

Zeke nodded dryly. He knew exactly what she meant.

"One barman we spoke to said he saw a fella like you on an Appaloosa headed south. We just follered our noses, I guess you could say, and we ended up ridin' through Booneville. Well, the whole town was riled up about a half-breed who kidnapped some rancher's wife. Said he rode an Appaloosa. Best we could figure, it was you and there was some misunderstandin'."

"Misunderstanding?" Lizzie cut in. "Hardly. That would be my father spreading lies again." She stepped closer to Jessie and Zeke, holding out a hand to Jessie.

Zeke thought it remarkable that even though his mother was dressed in far more feminine clothing than Jessie's checkered shirt and denim pants, there was little else that differed between the two women.

"I want to thank you both for what you've done for my son," Lizzie went on. "He's told me everything, how you took him in and made him part of your family. And the fact that you came looking for him, well, that says more than words ever could. If you hadn't arrived just now, I don't know what might have happened."

"I always knew Zeke came from good stock," Jessie said,

gripping Lizzie's hand. "And it's a downright pleasure to shake his real ma's hand."

"How about some formal introductions, Zeke?" Tanner said with a chuckle in his voice.

Zeke obliged, and the introductions were made. Walks With Bears translated for Rides The Sun and his wife, who then excused themselves.

"I wish also to spend some time with my wife alone," Walks With Bears said as his friend disappeared into the darkness. "You stay and tell your friends what has happened, Zeke. There is much they do not know."

"What if Sullivan comes back?" Zeke asked, still feeling a little shaken from the tense situation that had just occurred.

"We'll stay near the village," Lizzie promised him.

Zeke nodded and indicated to Jessie and Tanner to take a seat around the fire. They did, and he joined them, still watching his real parents disappear into the night beyond the reach of the firelight. "I never figured this day would come so quick," he said, running both hands through his hair as he sat down on a flat boulder. "I never figured my folks would have had so much working against 'em, neither."

"Looks a lot like providence to me," Jessie said.

Zeke looked at her for a moment, pondering her words. "Yeah, it sure was," he agreed and began to tell them how he had hit brick walls everywhere and finally just drifted eastward, not really knowing where he was going but hoping he would stumble upon someone who could point him in the right direction.

He told them how he had arrived at his father's village and been noticed by Rides The Sun. He was just relating his father's reaction when he first saw the silver bracelet as a muffled scream silenced him. Zeke sprang to his feet.

A muttered curse followed, and the next moment, Larry

Quick staggered into the circle of light cast by the fire, dragging Zeke's mother with him. He spun around and glared at Zeke, one arm around Lizzie's neck and the other hand pressing the barrel of a pistol against her temple. "Nobody crosses me and gets away with it. Especially not an all-fired half-breed," he spat venomously.

CHAPTER 11
DUEL

Zeke held his hands away from his guns, aware that Tanner and Jessie were doing the same. Just as Walks With Bears had said, Larry was a tight bowstring, ready to release its agent of death at the slightest provocation.

"I reckon you insulted me back there in Fountain," Larry said. "Beating my best horse with your spotted paint pony you annexed from some sorry soul. I said it wasn't the last you'd see of me, didn't I? Well, here I am."

Zeke caught Jessie's eye. She had that expressionless look on her face. The one that said, *I'm going to let you say everything you want to say until you get really comfortable and think you're in control.* Zeke decided to follow her lead.

"Now, you and me, half-breed, we're going face off in a duel. Man to man. Your clunky cannons there against my six-shooter. Either that, or I'll let you watch your sweet mama die right in front of you." Larry paused, apparently for effect.

Zeke stared at him unblinking, keeping his thoughts centered, his face bland.

"You yeller, half-breed? You need your Indian-lovin' friends to take care of your business for ya? Or you goin' t' show us what a real man does when he's in a tight spot?"

Zeke felt hot anger rushing through his veins. He couldn't keep quiet anymore. "I beat you fair and square in that race on my own horse. I was beating you fair and square when you fought me for no good reason. And as I recollect, it's you who was insultin' me. Like you are right now. But I ain't afraid of you. I beat you at everything else, I'll beat you at dueling, too, Mister Quick."

"Zeke! Don't let him draw you out!" Jessie cried out in a panicked voice.

"Ooh, listen to your mama, now," Larry wheedled.

"Shut up, you varmint," Jessie snapped back at him. "You can't be trusted to play fair. Zeke ain't duelin' the likes of you, no way, no how, you filthy sidewinder."

"I got to do this, Ma-Jess," Zeke said, not taking his eyes off Larry for a moment. The gunman was smiling like the sidewinder who got the eagle's egg. "I ain't the thirteen-year-old kid you took in. I'm a man now. I got to fight my own battles."

"But, Zeke," Jessie protested.

All Zeke could see were his real mother's frightened, yet defiant eyes and Larry Quick's gun pressed against her head. "I got to do this," he repeated a little louder. "Let her go, Larry! I said I'll duel ya!"

Larry gave a coarse laugh, spat on the ground, then shoved Lizzie away from him. She staggered toward the tipi, but Larry put a bullet in the ground in front of her feet before she could get there. She stopped. "You stay where I can see you, woman," he snapped.

"I got my Yellowboy trained on you, Quick," Jessie said without missing a beat. "You put away that six-gun of yours and set up for that duel you wanted. And you better not try any tricks. One false move and I'll send you straight to Hades."

Lizzie moved over to where Tanner and Jessie stood. Now that she was free and he could think of other things, Zeke found himself wondering where his father was. And for that matter, where his grandfather was. For a moment, he hesitated. Was this a ploy to keep him busy while Sullivan took revenge on Walks With Bears?

"Where's your boss, Larry?" he said.

"Takin' care of his own business while I take care of mine," Larry said, rearranging his gun belt around his waist. "We both got some payback coming due, I reckon."

Zeke didn't need any interpretation to know what Larry meant by payback. Both men had a score to settle, or so they believed. He felt sure Sullivan had his father. Quick and Sullivan had probably ambushed them, and each taken his prisoner. If Walks With Bears had escaped, he would have been back at the village already.

Zeke weighed his options, watching Larry select a piece of level ground to stand on. To the untrained eye, Larry might appear to be taking his time and looking distracted, but Zeke knew better. Every move was deliberate.

Quick was watching him, ready to put a bullet between his shoulder blades if he tried to duck out of the duel and go looking for his father. There was nothing for it. He would have to face off with Larry and get it over with. The sooner he did that, the sooner he could go looking for his father.

"All right, Quick, let's see you live up to your name," Zeke said, placing his feet slightly apart in the dirt and spitting on his hands. He rubbed them together, flexed his fingers and curled them into two fists, then shook them out. He could hear his pulse in his ears, feel his heartbeat in his throat. He shook his head and rolled it around to stretch out his neck muscles. Then he rolled back his shoulders and took a deep breath.

The sound of pulsing drums seemed to echo through his spirit in time with his heartbeat, along with chants of the Nez Percé. Chants that told of brave warriors, victorious in battle against the Shoshone and the Crow.

He felt himself grow calm, his vision clear and focused, his hands sure and steady. Time seemed to slow down all around him as he watched Larry slip his gun back into the holster and take up his stance opposite Zeke.

In that moment, all other sound and sight ceased to exist. Zeke could see Larry's eyes glittering in the firelight. Larry's eyelid twitched. The corner of his mouth lifted slightly. His eyes narrowed. When Zeke saw Larry Quick's hand begin to move toward the butt of his revolver, Zeke saw his own hand lift into the line of his sight, without being aware he had taken hold of the weapon.

As his hand came up, his thumb pulled back the hammer in one smooth motion, followed by the gentle squeeze on the trigger. The kick of the LeMat pulsed through his wrist even before he heard the boom of the explosion.

As fire erupted from the muzzle of his gun, he saw a flash of orange from Larry's weapon and almost instantly a searing pain shot through his thigh, as if someone had stabbed him with the wrong end of a red-hot branding iron. In that moment, Larry jerked backward and to his left, spinning around and landing face down in the dirt.

Zeke holstered his gun and stood looking at the man for a couple of heartbeats, then he turned away. "Ma," he said, walking to Lizzie's side. "Where's Pa? What did they do with him?"

Before he could reach his mother, he saw Jessie lifting her rifle, her eyes looking past him. Zeke instinctively fell flat.

Before the Yellowboy's muzzle had reached higher than Jessie's hip, the gun boomed, quickly followed by a report from Tanner's Colt Paterson. Behind him, Zeke heard a sharp cry and then a groan.

He knew what he would see before he even looked around. When the Nugents aimed at something, they seldom missed it. He heaved himself up, brushing dirt off his shirt, his heart aching more than his leg.

He turned slowly and saw Larry lying face up this time, his eyes staring unseeing into the dome of the night sky, his hands flung out to his sides, his legs awkwardly folded backward, and his feet under him. A large, dark stain was seeping through his shirt.

Zeke turned back to face Jessie. "I'm so sorry," he began and didn't know how to go on. Jessie's vow to never kill a man was all he could think of. Now, because of him, she had broken that vow. He should have aimed better. He should have made sure Larry was dead before he turned around.

"I ain't sorry, son," Jessie said, lowering the rifle once more. "I know what you're thinkin' and you got it backward. I didn't kill a man. He got himself killed. All I did was stop him killin' you."

Zeke stared at her. If only he could believe her. If only it was that simple.

Jessie seemed to know he needed more convincing. "What do you think'll weigh heaviest on my mind? Stoppin' that outlaw dead in his tracks or knowin' I could've saved your life but didn't 'cause of some vow I made?"

"But it ain't just some vow," Zeke protested, still feeling the heavy weight of regret and responsibility.

"Maybe so," Jessie agreed with a slight shrug. "But it ain't worth your life to me, Zeke."

Zeke nodded. It was all too much. He couldn't process it now.

"Now let's get you both cleaned up and took care of," Jessie said briskly.

The villagers had gathered around. Some were nudging the dead outlaw with their feet while others held back their children from going closer. There was much talking and gesturing. Rides The Sun pushed through the crowd and looked down on the corpse with a look of inevitability on his face. He caught Zeke's eye and nodded.

Jessie herded everyone into Walks With Bears's tipi. Rides The Sun stayed outside and chased away the curious villagers. Tanner took care of Zeke's wound, cauterizing it with a spear he found in the tipi heated to almost red hot in the fire. Larry's bullet had gone clean through the muscle and didn't seem to have hit any important blood vessels. Jessie took care of Lizzie, gently cleaning the wounds she had sustained being dragged across the stony, brush-covered ground.

"Zeke," Lizzie said, holding Jessie's hand still for a moment in its ministrations. "Sullivan took your pa. I'm afraid he'll kill him if he hasn't already."

Zeke would have jumped to his feet if Tanner hadn't held a firm restraining hand on his arm.

"You're in no shape to go hunting folks," he said. "Jessie and me, we'll go track 'em down soon as you two are taken care of."

"No!" Zeke declared stubbornly.

Jessie said, "Now, Zeke, use your head. You should stay here with Rides The Sun and take care of your ma until we get back. That old man's likely countin' on you being dead or comin' after him so he can finish what Larry didn't." She was patient with him, as she had always been, but even that didn't soften him.

"I come a long way to find my folks, with a heck of a lot of pushback," Zeke said, gritting his teeth as the hot metal of the spear seared the flesh of the exit wound in his leg. "I ain't sitting back now and letting someone else finish what I started. This is my battle. Mine and my pa's. I'll be danged if I leave him alone to fight without me ever again."

"It's dark, Zeke," Lizzie reminded him. "Sullivan could have taken Wally anywhere. He could be lying in wait for you."

"You folks are forgettin' something about me," Zeke said, getting to his feet and wincing at the stab of pain from the burned flesh and torn muscle fibers of his leg. "I survived seven years with an emigrant family who didn't want me. I was a slave for the Nez Percé for three years, and I spent another three years on the run, dodging angry farmers, lawmen, and outlaws. Even Indians, sometimes. I reckon I can handle myself." He was strapping his gun belt back on as he spoke. There was no way even Jessie was going to talk him out of this. He'd made up his mind.

"I am Cheyenne," Zeke added. "I stand by my kin. Is that too hard to understand?" He looked into his mother's eyes. If anyone there would understand, it had to be her. She had married a Cheyenne, after all. Lived in his tipi and bore his child.

"Yes," Lizzie said softly, her eyes full of understanding. "I do understand. Do what you need to do, my son."

Tears sprang to Zeke's eyes, and he blinked them away rapidly. There would be time enough for emotions afterward. He stepped over to Lizzie, kissed her on the top of her head, then turned and left the tipi without another word.

Outside, Rides The Sun was waiting for him. He held out a bear claw necklace that had four large fangs arranged in the front, between the rows of claws.

"Ného'e wear in battle. You wear now," he said.

Zeke nodded and allowed his father's best friend to fasten the necklace around his neck.

Rides The Sun placed a hand on Zeke's shoulder. "You go, Hotohkôhma'aestse. Maheo go with you."

He handed Zeke a knife made of bone, and Zeke thrust it into his belt. Rides The Sun must have gotten Hoedown ready for him because the horse was standing right there beside the tipi, his saddle on, his ears flicking back and forth as if he knew something was about to happen.

Zeke took the reins and a burning branch from the fire that Rides The Sun handed to him. Casting about in the direction he'd seen Larry drag his mother in from, he found himself frustrated by the many moccasin prints from the crowd that had gathered. Yet he kept on, holding the burning branch high, his eyes riveted to the ground, searching for some other mark.

Then he found it. Between the farthest lodges of the village, the clear sign of something heavy being dragged along the ground became visible. Lizzie had certainly put up a fight, digging her heels in and making as deep a gouge in the earth as she could. It was easy to follow that.

Zeke mounted up and began to follow the sign. He still held the burning branch in his hand, lighting the ground ahead. Soon he would have to put the fire out when he came closer to the place where his mother and father had been drygulched. It wouldn't be smart to advertise his approach.

He began to wonder what he would find. Somewhere at the end of this trail would be another trail—or his father. Perhaps alive, perhaps dead. There was only one way to find out for sure and that was to follow that trail, wherever it led him. Inside him, a growing sense of foreboding filled his chest.

He might not be certain of what he would find, but one thing he seemed to know with uncanny certainty: whatever he found would not leave him the same. He wasn't sure he was ready for the change.

CHAPTER 12
THE HANGING ROAD

The first thing Walks With Bears became aware of was pain. Overwhelming, nauseating pain. His head throbbed, every inch of him burned and ached all at once. Then he realized with cold shock that his nose and mouth were full of water.

He jerked his head upward and began to cough, raking in great gulps of air in between. Holding his head up out of the icy cold water he found himself lying face down in, he peered into the darkness around him, trying to figure out where he was and what had happened to him.

Slowly becoming aware of himself and his surroundings, Walks With Bears had the sensation of movement and realized he was being dragged along bodily. He could hear a horse walking through a river or a creek. His hands were reaching out above his head. He tried to pull them down, but soon it became clear that his wrists were tied.

Looking up, Walks With Bears saw the hind quarters of a horse in the moonlight above him. The rope around his wrists extended across those haunches to what must be a saddle horn.

He tried to wriggle his hands free from the bonds, but they

were too tight. The horse was walking, thankfully, though it still felt as if Walks With Bears's arms were being pulled out of their sockets. With gargantuan effort, he struggled to his feet, stumbling along in the shallows of the creek, and grabbed the rope higher up. Hauling on it with all his effort, he brought the horse to a standstill.

Then he collapsed on his back in the creek, letting the cold water run over him and trying to remember how he had ended up in this predicament. Closing his eyes, he searched his memory, grasping the fragments of incidents as they popped up in his mind.

The first thing he remembered, with a flood of emotion, was Lizzie. Lizzie had come home with Red Star, or Zeke. Sullivan and his gunman had arrived after dark, and Zeke's friends had helped get rid of them. He and Lizzie had gone for a walk together to be alone. He could remember wanting to find out whether she was still the same Lizzie he had loved, or if time had changed her.

They hadn't gone very far when he'd heard a rustling behind him and turned to see who or what was there. Something hard hit him on the side of his head. After that, he had no memory. He lay still, letting the water wash over him, aware that the horse was shifting its weight on the rocky creek bed.

Walks With Bears deliberately slowed his breathing, counting methodically and silently to five for each inhalation and each exhalation, allowing his body to come awake through the fog of pain and reconnect with his mind.

Gradually, the pain became bearable, though he knew it was most likely because he was simply getting used to it. An unconscious man dragged behind a horse could sustain many grievous wounds. Before he could take care of them, though, he needed to be in full control of his mind and body.

"You know, your people are a curse on the earth," a low male voice said in the darkness.

Walks With Bears's eyes flew open. He rolled onto his side and crouched in the water, feeling for his knife. It wasn't there in his belt where it usually was. In hindsight, that was no surprise at all. No kidnapper in his right mind was going to leave his victim armed.

"You're worse than dogs."

Walks With Bears knew that voice. It was Sullivan. He should have known Lizzie's father would do something like this. All at once, his mind began to run in circles. Sullivan had trussed him up and dragged him behind a horse. Where was Lizzie? Had he tied her up somewhere? Did Larry have her? What were they doing to her? He began to pick at the ropes around his wrists with his teeth, anxious to be free. Sullivan was still talking, though Walks With Bears could not see him. If Sullivan could see Walks With Bears, he did not seem to be worried that he was trying to get away.

"You Cheyenne and your friends the Arapaho, slaughtering and burning, everywhere you go. Killing women and children all over Colorado Territory, ignoring treaties your own chiefs signed. You know what's the matter with you? You can't keep your word. Say one thing and do entirely another. That's how you operate."

The hemp fibers of the rope were gorged with water, making them thick and unyielding. Walks With Bears's jaw and teeth ached, adding to the throbbing that coursed through his body. It was clear he was getting nowhere with the knots. Instead, he searched for a sharp-edged boulder somewhere in the river. There had to be one. He had to get free.

"I've heard it said your kind likes making war. You think fighting is exhilarating, entertainment. Your trouble is you have no respect for life. None whatsoever."

Walks With Bears stopped running his hands over the rocks and boulders in the creek. "Respect for life?" he echoed, looking in the direction of Sullivan's voice.

"Yes, respect for life. I don't expect you to know what that means, savage as you are." Sullivan's words were sarcastic, his tone derisive.

Walks With Bears drew a long, deep breath. "Did your Colonel Chivington know what that means? Respect for life?" he asked, keeping his tone as even as he could. He would not be drawn into a shouting match with the man, but he would also not sit by and let this White man paint his people with a tarred brush.

"And what of the many others who set off wars for the sake of a single cow. They do not ask who did it. They say it must be the Indian, and so they kill every one they see or they kidnap an Indian and his family, demanding the return of a cow and accusing the man of lying when he says it was not his people who took the cow."

A movement caught Walks With Bears's eye.

Sullivan was standing up on the bank, his lean, slightly stooped outline rising from the earth against the star-studded sky. He was most likely armed, and Walks With Bears was not, but the latter could not stop himself from speaking.

"You say my people slaughter the White man's women and children. And I cannot say it is a lie. I am sure there are some who have done such things. But I wonder if you know how many of my people's women and children your big White chief's armies have killed? I speak not only of Black Kettle's camp. Many more times this has been done. You speak like one who is disgusted by these things, but only when an Indian is the one holding the gun."

"Shut your smart mouth, you dog!" Sullivan barked. "I'm not here to argue with you. I'm here to tell you this is your last warning. You stay away from Lizzie, or I'll make sure you join your ancestors in the happy hunting ground. Understood?"

"Happy hunting ground," Walks With Bears repeated tiredly. "This place you speak of does not exist except in the White man's imagination. You know nothing of the First Nations of this land. You know nothing of the real reasons behind the wars of this land."

"I don't give a continental! I said I'm not here to debate with you," Sullivan snapped. "You stay away from Lizzie, or you die. I'm taking her back home where she belongs."

What was wrong with the old man? Did he not understand his own language, spoken by his own daughter? It was clear she wished not to be where her father was. It was very clear she had never wished to be married to the man her father had forced upon her.

Weariness gave way to frustration and frustration to anger. The hot lava of indignation running through Walks With Bears seemed to numb his pain even more, though it made his temples throb.

"You waste your words, Sullivan," he said deliberately, clenching his bound hands. "Lizzie has made her choice. I also have made my choice. We are married and we have a son."

Sullivan sighed audibly. He walked away a few steps. Then he turned and came back. "You leave me no option but to put an end to you right now, you fool. And that's probably better anyway since I'm sure Larry has already dispatched your bastard son. You'll probably come after me to avenge his death, anyway."

The words hit Walks With Bears like a war club in the face. Not so much the insinuation that Red Star was illegitimate, but that Larry had killed him. He'd heard that word, "dispatched," used before in such situations, and he knew what it meant.

"You hire a man to kill your own grandson?" Walks With

Bears almost choked on the words. "You have no honor to face him yourself?"

"Grandson? You didn't hear me, did you? I said he's your bastard son. He's nothing of mine."

"Red Star is no bastard!" Walks With Bears said forcefully, not sure where he was getting the strength but giving vent to his anger and frustration. "Lizzie is my wife. We vowed to be faithful in a sacred ceremony that you did not attend because you chose it so."

"You stole my daughter," Sullivan insisted stubbornly.

"In my culture, it is accepted to steal a bride, if the bride so wishes, though sometimes it is frowned upon." Walks With Bears wasn't sure why, but he wanted this man to understand. It could only be that he knew Sullivan's history and wished to help him heal and forget the pain of his loss. He was still Lizzie's father, after all. In the depths of his being, Walks With Bears felt an inexplicable urge to have Sullivan's blessing on their marriage.

"Culture? What culture is that?" Sullivan spat derisively.

"The same culture that says a woman may leave her husband if he raises his hand to her." Walks With Bears said slowly. "You do not want your daughter stolen, but you are happy to sell her, like a slave. You know the Bennet man beats her, but you look away and speak of other things because you love money more than you love your own flesh and blood."

Cold silence was all that came from Sullivan's looming shadow.

Walks With Bears decided to give the final thrust of truth. "And you are surprised because Lizzie does not wish to stay with you and your Bennet but rather wishes to live with a wild savage like me. Perhaps it is because I and my people treat her the way a woman needs to be treated. Perhaps this is why she loves me, a stranger and a dog, and not her own father."

For a moment longer, the icy silence remained hanging in the air. Then a low roar began to rumble in Sullivan's chest, erupting into incoherent shouting as the white-haired old man strode down the bank and began striking Walks With Bears with his horse whip across the face.

Raising his tied hands, the Cheyenne warrior covered his face, trying to protect it from the blows. His fingers were already numb, the blood being cut off by the thick, swollen ropes around his wrists, but he could feel the whip cutting the flesh of his arms.

The next minute, Sullivan pulled a pistol out of from under his coat, gripped it by the muzzle, and began beating Walks With Bears about his head and torso.

The Cheyenne stood to his feet, every muscle and tendon screaming with the effort and agony. There was little he could do to defend himself, but if he kept moving, he would be able to at least dodge some of the blows until he found a way to escape or until Sullivan grew tired and stopped. Or shot him.

It might have worked if Walks With Bears hadn't been dragged by a horse for many miles. Or if Sullivan had not been so filled with rage and determined to inflict as much damage as he possibly could.

As it was, Walks With Bears could not manage to avoid a single wild blow of Sullivan's gun. He had to face the truth that he could not get away. Instead, he would have to stand his ground and fight.

All he had to fight with was his bound hands. It put him at disadvantage. A bit like the dog rope he had used when he fought as a younger man. The knowledge that the decorated sash pinned him to the ground, giving him a limited area to fight in, and prevented him from running away from the fight, had somehow heightened his awareness, sharpened his senses.

Perhaps the rope around his wrists could give him a similar

advantage. Gathering his wits, Walks With Bears timed the lift of Sullivan's hand as it readied itself for the next blow. Just as the man exposed his torso, Walks With Bears balled both fists and rammed them into Sullivan's midriff. The older man wheezed, the pistol in his hand dropping down like a dead fish onto Walks With Bears's back.

Sullivan staggered backward. "Blast it!" he rasped, gasping for the wind he just had knocked out of him.

Walks With Bears took advantage of the moment of respite, stepping backward. If he could not loosen the rope around his wrists, he would untie it from the pommel horn and use it as a weapon.

He staggered to the horse, aware he was fading in and out of consciousness and fighting the black curtain of oblivion. He had just managed to untie the loops of twisted hemp around the saddle horn when something hard connected with his left shoulder blade.

Walks With Bears swung around, once again clenching his fists but this time using his forearms like a club. Sullivan might not have been a young man anymore, but he was wiry, and he was strong. He had also not been dragged along the rocky ground for untold miles behind a horse. Most of all, he seemed to have wizened up to the fact that Walks With Bears was not going take his beating lying down.

Sullivan dodged Walks With Bears's swing and caught the rope trailing from the Cheyenne's wrists, jerking his arms back and toppling him off balance. Walks With Bears fell against the horse, trying desperately to stay on his feet, but the animal snorted and shied, and the warrior found himself making painful contact with the ground once more.

A boot crunched on gravel. Sullivan grunted. Walks With Bears opened his eyes in time to see a leather missile aimed at his head. He lifted his arms again, shielding his face. Sullivan's boot connected with his arms and sent stabs of pain all the way down into his back muscles. Walks With Bears tried to roll away from what he was sure would be another brutal kick but was suddenly unable to move.

Time seemed to stand still. He could see the stars suspended above him. The hanging road unfurled its carpet of silver beads against a night sky as black as war paint, seeming to beckon him to follow it into the realm of the unknown to the camp of the dead. He resisted its pull. He couldn't go. Not yet. Not with a wife and son who needed him.

The sound of the shot ringing out all around had no effect on him, though he heard it. It seemed to be coming from another world.

Vainly, he tried to lift his head, pull himself away from the dark whirlpool of cold silence that was threatening to suck him under. He tried to feel where the bullet had hit him, but his whole body was either numb or throbbing with pain. There was no fresh burn of agony searing through him.

The stars above him seemed to grow brighter and brighter until they melted together in a blaze of brilliant light. Walks With Bears closed his eyes against it, but nothing helped. He lay still, weighed down by an invisible iron blanket pinning him to the ground.

"I cannot go yet, Maheo." He felt his cracked lips mouthing the whispered words. "Please, let me stay. For Lizzie. For Red Star."

CHAPTER 13
BLOOD AND WATER

Zeke slowly lowered his hand, feeling slightly sick to his stomach. The smell of burned gun powder smoke clawed at his nostrils, but he hardly noticed it.

The LeMat in his right hand felt heavier than usual, but he couldn't gather his thoughts sufficiently to holster the weapon again.

There in front of him, on the ground a few feet away, lay his father's still form. The creek babbled onward, unperturbed, it's journey along the valley floor not in the least affected by the blood spilled on its banks.

By contrast, Zeke's world had just come to a grinding standstill. In the pale, bluish light of the moon, Zeke couldn't really see well enough to tell whether his father's ribs were still rising and falling. All he knew was he lay deathly still.

In his peripheral vision, Zeke could see Sullivan staggering backward, gasping and clutching at his chest. The gun he had been using to beat Walks With Bears lay gleaming and impotent on the ground.

Zeke felt numb. Hollow. He couldn't remember when he decided to shuck his weapon and shoot. He couldn't even remember if he'd made any kind of decision at all or if he had simply acted on instinct.

Sullivan fell in an undignified heap on the ground and sat there, still holding his chest with both hands. His rasping breaths and wheezing moans cut through the deathly stillness left after the report of Zeke's bullet faded away.

Zeke stared at him for a while then down at the LeMat in his hand. Slowly, he brought it back to the holster and slid it into the leather casing. In that moment, the reality of what he had just seen, and just done, dawned upon him in a burst of clarity.

Raw, wild rage surged up in his throat. He gripped the handle of the bone knife that Rides The Sun had given him. As his fingers closed around the deer horn grip, he felt as if he were watching himself from outside.

Drawing the knife, he ran over to Sullivan and grabbed the man's silvery forelock in his left hand. Sullivan yelped but didn't say a word. His breathing came in short, rasping bursts.

"You killed my father!" Zeke screamed in Sullivan's face, although he himself could hardly breathe. His chest felt so tight, his lungs were burning. "Now you will pay with your life!"

He stared into the old man's eyes with the moonlight reflected in them. There was no flintiness in them now, no self-assured pride, no disdain or hatred, only a desperate desire to live and a crippling fear of death. The events of the previous six weeks marched in a procession of memories through Zeke's mind.

At last, he had found his father and his mother. Found them miles apart and yet still connected by a special thread called love. By some miracle, he had managed to bring them together and, in the process, found out who he was and discovered he was loved and wanted, that he belonged, not to one or the other culture but to both. He was Lizzie's boy, and he was Walks With Bears's son.

He was Cheyenne and he was European. He was the old world and the new, dancing in perfect synchronization, singing in perfect harmony. He was Red Star, and he was Zeke Nugent.

And now this old man, who was supposed to be his blood kin, had killed the one person in the world most dear to him. Before he had time to learn to know him, to see into his heart and find those things he shared with him. The things that made them who they were: father and son.

The spear point of knowing what he had found and lost in such quick succession pierced his heart, unleashing a guttural, violent cry from his belly. Rage coursed through him like a swollen mountain river in springtime, fed by the cumulative waters of melting snow and ice.

Raising the bone knife high into the air, he gripped Sullivan's hair tighter, jerking the man's forehead upward, ready for the knife to sweep down and do its job.

"Red Star! Stop!"

The voice was weak, but it's emphasis was strong. As strong as the heart behind it. Zeke did not need to turn around to know it was his father's voice. Walks With Bears was alive? Or was it his ghost speaking?

Zeke stared down at Sullivan. The old man's eyes stared back, filled with confusion and horror. The knife hovered above them both, white and menacing in the moonlight.

"No son of mine will scalp his own grandfather."

Zeke felt as if he had just woken up. The white hair gripped in his fist felt at once like a handful of hot coals. He unclenched his fist and stepped back, bringing his knife hand harmlessly to his side. His heart pounded in his ears, and only then did he realize he was breathing hard, as if he had just run clear across the Great American Desert.

Sullivan slumped down and seemed to be crying.

Zeke turned around to see Walks With Bears trying to sit up. He walked to his father as if in a dream and reached out to him. Just then, he saw the torn and bloodied deerskin pants, the cuts on his father's forearms, the gash on the side of his head. He stopped, afraid to touch him and cause more pain. "Ného'e!" he said in a hoarse whisper. "What did he do to you?"

Walks With Bears didn't reply. Instead, he held out his hands, and Zeke saw the thick coils of rope. The knife was still in his hand, and it took him only a moment to cut his father free. "Cut these clothes off me and help me to the creek. The cold water will clean my wounds, so the flesh does not rot."

Zeke decided to let his father take hold of him to steady himself. Obediently, he cut the deerskin trousers and tunic from Walks With Bears's body and walked slowly beside him to the creek, his father leaning on his shoulder for support. Walks With Bears lay down in a rock pool.

"Now take Sullivan to the village. Perhaps it is not too late to save his life."

Zeke started and almost tripped over a rock in the water. "Save his life? A man who hates you so much he tried to kill you?"

"Ah, Red Star..." Walks With Bears smiled a tight, agonized smile. "You have not learned from your father's mistakes. Revenge has been our people's way for many winters, but that does not mean it is the right way. Revenge brings no peace. It adds more pain to a heart already broken."

Zeke hardly dared look over at Sullivan. His breathing was still rasping on the cold air but seemed to be slowing. "What if I don't make it in time?" he asked. "I shot him in the chest, Ného'e."

"Yes, but I hear him breathing. If he is not dead yet, the bullet did not enter his heart. There is still hope. Go now. If anything kills Theo Sullivan, let it be his own hatred and not his grandson's bullet."

Zeke hesitated only a moment longer. Part of him wanted to ignore the wheezing old man, leave him to the fate he had brought upon himself, but his father's words rang in his spirit, and he knew he could not do it.

Perhaps the fact his bullet had not found Sullivan's heart was because he had not really wanted it to. As heartbroken and enraged as he had been a moment ago, the overriding truth was that he had no desire to kill. Not even someone like Sullivan.

"I'm leaving one LeMat with you. In case you need it," he said, unbuckling one of the guns from his gun belt and laying it down on a boulder near his father. Then he walked over to Hoedown, removed his bedroll, and laid it on the bank within easy reach for his father.

Taking a deep breath, he turned back to Sullivan. The old man was now a frail, shrunken version of himself, coughing spasmodically, his chin dark and shining with blood. Zeke ripped a sleeve off Sullivan's shirt and dipped it in the creek. Then he plugged the hole in his grandfather's chest and helped him up onto his horse.

"Just you hang over like a pair of saddlebags. Let the blood run out your mouth instead of gathering in your lung," Zeke advised.

Sullivan meekly accepted that advice. The next moment, hoof beats filled the air. Zeke hesitated before mounting his horse and looked across the saddle to see who was coming.

"Zeke? You all right? We heard the gunshot." It was Tanner.

Zeke couldn't remember ever being happier to see the steady, unaffected cowboy-turned-homesteader riding up. "Yeah. We're all right. Well, sort of. We need to get Sullivan to the village. He needs help." He couldn't bring himself to say out loud that he had shot his own grandfather, though he knew, at some point, they would all know the whole truth. There would be time enough for telling the story. First, they had a life to save.

"Sure thing." Tanner's response was comfortingly predictable.

"Matter of fact, could you take care of that for me, Pa-Tanner?" Zeke asked. "I'd rather stay here with my pa."

"Of course."

Zeke handed Sullivan's horse's reins over to Tanner and watched him ride off with the groaning, wheezing patient. He felt suddenly weak, as if all his bones had turned to calf's foot jelly. Leaning against Hoedown's solid, warm shoulder, he looked up into the starry night sky and let the tears roll silently down his cheeks.

ZEKE WALKED into the village the next morning, leading Hoedown with his father in the saddle. Walks With Bears was wrapped in Zeke's blanket. He looked tired, but his eyes were bright with hope and pride. Lizzie ran out to meet them, tearful but happy to see them both still breathing.

After Zeke helped Walks With Bears down out of the saddle, Lizzie took over from there. With his arm over her shoulders, she all but carried him into the tipi, already telling him of the salves and poultices she had made, ready to treat his wounds.

Jessie walked up to Zeke and put both hands on his shoulders. It was the closest she ever came to giving him a hug. It was the closest he ever came to letting her give him one.

"I sure am proud of you, son," she said, her eyes warm with affection. Then she coughed. "You know, now that you found your own blood folks, I reckon there's really no need t' go on calling us Ma and Pa," she said. "Doesn't seem right no more."

Zeke tilted his head to one side. "Can I call you Cattle Kate, like the fellers from the Lightfoot Gang did?"

Jessie looked up sharply, her face registering shock and a little indignation. She looked like she was about to give a sharp retort when Zeke's grin and irrepressible chuckle stopped her. "You little varmint, you!" she cried, though she was smiling as she thumped him on the shoulder. "You sure had me going for a moment, there! I declare!"

Zeke laughed. "I'll see about what to call you folks. For now, ain't nothing changing what y'all did for me when I had no family and no future. Sometimes blood ain't thicker'n water."

"I reckon," Jessie said, her eyes giving Zeke a good going over.

He knew she was assessing his state and determining whether he needed mothering.

"Right now, you better get something thicker'n water inside your belly before you end up eatin' dirt. You look like death warmed over. Now, I already got a pan bread goin' on the fire, and soon as that's out, I'll fix you the biggest omelet you ever did see." As she spoke, she began putting her words into action.

Zeke watched her bustling around the fire and smiled to himself. He sure was uncommonly lucky, having two families who cared for him so much. Maybe the good Lord was making up for everything he'd been robbed of during the first thirteen-odd years of his life.

When he and Jessie and Tanner sat down to eat, and Lizzie took food inside the tipi for herself and Walks With Bears, Zeke finally plucked up the courage to ask about Sullivan. Jessie looked at Tanner. Tanner nodded slowly and finished chewing the bread and omelet in his mouth. Then he took a swig of coffee and shifted on the log he sat on so that he could look directly at Zeke.

Zeke's heart thudded in his ears. He had cooled down

considerably since the night before, and now the unthinkable had him by the gullet. He understood now, better than ever before, why Jessie had made that vow never to kill a man.

When he had hooked up with the Lightfoot Gang, he'd watched them kill men without so much as blinking and thought it must give a fellow a great sense of power to end the life of another living being. Especially one that was doing you harm or threatened your life.

Now that he faced the possibility that his bullet might have taken the life of his grandfather, no matter how hateful and murderous the old man had been, Zeke didn't feel so powerful after all. He had spent the entire night thinking about it while he sat guard over his father, lying in the creek.

In truth, it was fear that had made him pull the trigger. Fear and hatred and an overwhelming, sickening sense of helplessness and impotence all wrapped up in a fiery rage over which he had no control.

He had always thought gunmen were strong and in control, but he knew the truth now. It was not strong men who killed other men. It was weak or desperate men who did that. He didn't want to be either of those things.

"The good news is that bullet didn't sever anything too serious," Tanner said, breaking in on Zeke's thoughts. "Missed the heart, too, but I figure you knew that already."

Zeke nodded mutely. If that was the good news, he wondered what the bad news was.

"Right now, Sullivan's out cold. He's still breathin', but he's pretty much burnin' up with fever. I won't lie to ya, Zeke. It's touch and go is what it is. The folks here know their way around this kind of thing, an' they're for sure doin' everything they can. But only time will tell, I'm afraid."

Zeke nodded dumbly. For now, he was in the clear.

"You can pray for him, ya know?" Jessie said softly.

Zeke looked sharply at her. Would God even listen to him? Jessie's eyes told him she knew what was going on in his mind, and she wasn't going to go back on what she had just said.

Zeke went back to eating. Only now that he was putting food in his mouth did he realize how hungry he was. He wolfed everything down and then went and sat under a clump of yellowwood trees and watched the herd of village horses grazing.

The leaves were beginning to turn golden and some were falling, drifting slowly down and settling on the ground. As he watched them fall, he pleaded silently for God to spare the life of his grandfather.

Zeke didn't know how long he sat there before he fell asleep. When he woke, it was late afternoon, and someone was calling his name. He looked up, feeling groggy and disoriented.

Jessie came running toward him, waving her hat in the air. "He's awake, Zeke! He's askin' for ya!"

It took Zeke a moment to cotton to what she was talking about. Then it hit him. It had to be Sullivan. For a moment, Zeke felt paralyzed. Sure, he was relieved his grandfather was awake. That had to be a good sign. But how would he look into the eyes of a man he had almost scalped less than twenty-four hours ago?

Jessie reached his side, her cheeks flushed, her eyes bright with hope. She looked at him, and he could see she knew, once again, exactly what was going on inside his head. It was as unsettling as it was comforting, sometimes.

"Come on, then. You both of you got some apologizin' to do. May as well get on with it," she said with her mothering smile.

Zeke looked down and grunted, "Yeah."

He followed her back to the village, to the lodge of the old woman who had recognized Lizzie when they first came in and happened to be the village doctor, of sorts. The place was hot with steam and smelled of pungent herbs and fragrant leaves.

Sullivan lay on his side, the wounded lung uppermost. He was wrapped in skins dark with poultices and oils and covered with buffalo robes. In his hand was a wooden cup, holding a mixture that must have tasted horrible if the look on his face was anything to go by.

Lizzie was there, too, her face a picture of bittersweet relief. Jessie remained outside. The old woman, named simply Heseeota'e, meaning Herb Woman, ushered Zeke closer to Sullivan. Zeke could hardly bear to look at his grandfather, but he sat down on the buffalo robe beside Lizzie and stared at his hands.

Sullivan set down the cup, and Zeke could feel the old man's eyes on him. A war was raging inside his heart. On the one hand, he felt a compelling need to ask his grandfather's forgiveness. On the other, he felt he owed him no explanations. After all, the bullet in Sullivan's lung had saved the life of Zeke's father.

"Why did you spare my life?" Sullivan asked, his voice weak and raspy.

Zeke looked up. Of all the things he might have expected Sullivan to say, this was not one of them.

"You could have just left me to die, but you didn't. I don't understand that."

Zeke stared into his grandfather's piercing blue eyes. There was something different about them now. Something that looked a lot like humility. And guilt. Perhaps a little shame. The exact same things Zeke had been feeling only hours before.

He hadn't really known why it was he hadn't gone ahead and killed Sullivan, but now he knew, without the shadow of a doubt. "Like my pa said, ain't no son of his going to scalp his own grandpa."

CHAPTER 14
LEGACY

Springtime had never looked so good to Zeke. The promise of fresh life and new beginnings felt especially close to home this particular year. It made him feel a little heady, as if he were walking in a dream he didn't want to wake up from. He was washing in the same creek his father had cleansed his wounds on that horrible night that had turned everything around.

Strange how things sometimes had to come down to their very worst before they could get better. That was a thought he might want to hold onto for future reference. A stitch in time saves nine, Jessie loved to say. Zeke had a better idea now that it had less to do with sewing and more to do with life.

While he washed, Zeke's thoughts drifted over the events that had followed the night he almost scalped his grandfather. Sullivan's complete turnaround and change of heart had seemed almost too good to be true, until he had offered to be the one to tell Blake Bennet that he had no claim on Elizabeth since she had already been married when they had said their arranged vows.

"But what'll you tell him about not having an heir?" Lizzie had asked, her face strained with worry.

"I'll just have to tell him the truth, won't I?" Sullivan had replied stoically. "Why put another young woman through the hell I put you through?"

"He ain't goin' t' take that too well, I reckon," Jessie had chipped in. "Might decide to take it out on you for lyin' to him all these years."

"I thought of that," Sullivan had replied.

"Tanner and me don't mind goin' with ya, just to back you up."

Zeke could still see his grandfather waving off Jessie's offer. "You're very kind, but I must face the music myself. After all, I made up my bed, I better bloody well lie in it."

"What if he shoots you, Father? Or has you killed. You know what a temper Bennet has." Lizzie's face had told Zeke and anyone who saw her in that moment that Blake Bennet's temper was a fearsome thing to behold.

Sullivan had reached out and awkwardly patted his daughter's hand. "To be perfectly honest, I suppose I deserve nothing less. But if he does dispatch me, well, at least this time I have a chance of making it into heaven."

Thinking back, Zeke smiled at the memory and how, when they received a letter a couple of months later, his grandfather had declared he was still alive, though considerably less well off, and promised he would come visit Lizzie and her family on the reservation after the winter.

Now that spring was in full bloom, Zeke hoped the old man would make good on his promise. And a few other people who had promised to return, too.

He quickly finished his ablutions and dressed in a pair of deerskin leggings and tunic his mother had made for him under the watchful eyes of the other women in the tribe. They had accepted his mother as one of their own, helping her make clothing for herself and her family, showing her how they tended the crops and the cattle.

Zeke and his father sometimes went on short hunting trips, although there was not a lot of game and they had to be careful not to stray too far into the areas where the other tribes lived. On their first hunting trip of the springtime, they had met up with a troop of young Kiowa boys who boasted of an extended hunting range to the southwest of the Indian Territory, stretching beyond the shared lands of the Kiowa, Comanche, and Apache nations and where there were not many settlers.

Zeke wondered if the young Kiowas' parents would be happy their sons had told their sworn enemies of their tribe's hunting range, but he soon forgot about that, looking forward to the more extended hunting trips he and Walks With Bears were planning for the summer.

It was as if he were being given a second chance at truly understanding the ways of his Cheyenne heritage. With these thoughts drifting contentedly through his mind, he walked back to the village and found his mother busy preparing breakfast.

"You are just in time to welcome our guests," Lizzie said and then tried the same sentence in Cheyenne. Zeke laughed but knew he wouldn't do too much of a better job.

They were both still learning and liked to practice on each other. Walks With Bears was a patient teacher as well as a good father. His family repaid him by teaching him more of their language and introducing him to the works of great English writers.

Only when Zeke stepped into the tipi did he realize what his mother had meant by guests. Tanner and Jessie were seated opposite his father around the fire, puffing on a pipe that they passed between them.

Jubilant greetings were exchanged, followed by carefully selected gifts. Jessie had brought some more books, as well as candies and thick brown sugar, while Tanner had made a leather sheath for Zeke's bone knife. It fit perfectly.

"You'll join the races today?" Zeke asked, looking pointedly at Jessie.

"Wouldn't miss it for the world," Jessie said.

She made good on her promise, turning out to be the star attraction of the day. The young Cheyenne men had seen women ride, shoot, hunt, and even raid, but not White women. Especially not White women dressed like cowboys.

It was an idyllic day, filled with laughter and the thrills and spills of bareback racing and shooting competitions. Hoedown did his bit and flashed his spotted hindquarters at every horse he raced against, and Jessie impressed everyone present with her marksmanship.

By the time midday came around and the youngsters headed back to their parents' lodges to escape the heat of the day, Zeke was flushed and happy. He approached the family's tipi to find Tanner and his father deep in conversation while something that looked like a small deer roasted on a spit over the fire. Zeke sat down beside them, pulling out his bone knife from its new sheath and cutting a sliver of meat from the spit.

"It is a thing like the seasons," Walks With Bears was saying. "It cannot be stopped. One civilization rises while another is swallowed up in it. I have read it in your books that Red Star teaches me with. Rome, Greece, and what is the other one? Ah, yes, Egypt. Their power was far greater than the Cheyenne, or even the Comanche—called the lords of the plains—and yet they are no longer the powers they were."

Tanner looked pensive, a little sad even. "That don't mean it's all right if your people just up and disappear. You folks and the other First Nations, you've got your own territories. Who knows, maybe you'll even be able t' be a republic in your own right someday, like Texas was before it got annexed."

Walks With Bears laughed good humoredly. "Annexed? That is a word for stealing, yes?"

Tanner laughed along with his friend. "Yeah, to some folks it is. There's some that say the United States stole a whole country and called it annexing just to make it sound better."

"They will annex our land, too. You will see," Walks With Bears said quietly but without malice or self-pity.

"The White people become more and more. Their ways change faster than the Indian's. We love our old ways, but the White man is always looking for new ways. I do not know which is good or which is bad. Perhaps they are neither good nor bad but only different."

Zeke stopped chewing the meat in his mouth, his attention riveted on his father.

"What I do know is they cannot exist together in one place, the old ways, and the new ways. The one will swallow up the other. Soon our people will dress like the White man, live in the same houses, eat the same food, live the same way. If we do not, we will die. It is the only way."

Resistance pulsed through Zeke's veins. He didn't want to hear such things. He loved his Cheyenne heritage, and now his father was saying it would one day all be gone.

"How can you speak this way, Ného'e?" he said. "Our people are strong and proud. We know who we are. Do you have no hope for our future?"

"I have hope for our future but not for our old ways," Walks With Bears said. "I dreamed it, my son. I saw us on these reservations, and they shrank smaller and smaller until they were just little puddles. Puddles of firewater where no crops grow, and no cattle walk and the people sit and beg the big White chief for corn to grind."

Zeke wanted to make his father take it all back. It had to be a lie, or a mistake at least. Surely, they could go on hunting in the dry areas where the White man could not make his farms work. Surely this new and happy life he was living was not going to be snatched away from him as he had been snatched from his family as a helpless baby.

"Stop this talk. I do not want to hear it!" he said in Cheyenne.

Walks With Bears placed his hand on his son's shoulder. The weight of it spoke louder to Zeke's heart than any words his father might have uttered.

"My son, I speak this way, not because I have no hope but because I have found something new to put my hope in."

Zeke looked up into his father's deep, black eyes. They were so full of peace. It was clear to Zeke that Walks With Bears was not pretending.

"As a father and a Cheyenne, I have two choices. I can rage against the changes and resist the swallowing up of my nation into the new nation they call America. But I fear that will cause more pain than it heals. There is one other choice I have. I can pour all the strength and the wisdom of my people into my son and make him a man who walks among many nations, unashamed but able to adapt, able to learn new skills I never knew, and survive in a wilderness I will never see."

Walks With Bears's hand felt as hot as fire on Zeke's shoulder. His words were like arrows piercing deep into the young man's mind and soul.

"Your English books speak of a thing called legacy. I have learned much about this thing, and I have decided it is something I must give you, Red Star. If I can teach you and train you to be a just, humble, wise man, then you will also be a great man one day. A great man who brings changes in his world. Then I will watch from the camp of the dead and know that I have left a great legacy in my son. A legacy that will not only preserve our culture but change the world." Tears glittered in Walks With Bears's eyes.

Zeke's own eyes were smarting, and he blinked rapidly.

"Your father is very wise, young man. I'd advise you to learn everything you can from him. Every last thing."

Zeke spun around.

An old man stood there, dressed in a black broadcloth suit. His hair was silver-white, his blue eyes piercing but calm, his posture erect and proud but not aggressive.

"Grandpa!" Zeke cried.

"Now, don't go hugging me or any of that nonsense," Sullivan said, taking a small step back when Zeke rushed toward him. As he spoke, Sullivan held out his hand.

Zeke took it and pumped it vigorously. "Ma! Come look! It's Grandpa!" All the while, Zeke stared into his grandfather's face, reading the joy written there, even though Sullivan maintained what his grandson and son-in-law had since learned was referred to as a stiff upper lip.

Lizzie emerged from the tipi, her face the picture of happiness. "Father! What a wonderful surprise!"

"Yule said I'd better come out here and say hello before I get too old to travel," Sullivan said, giving Lizzie his hand and gripping hers tightly. "Your brother sends his regards, by the way. Managed to get a job as an Indian agent for the Ute. He's thinking of asking for a transfer here, so you might see more of him soon."

"And you, Father? Will we see more of you?"

Sullivan shrugged. "Guess I'll have to move where my children move, won't I?"

"You better, Grandpa!" Zeke said, dodging the cuff on the ear he had fully expected.

"Besides, a grandfather needs to be near his grandchild so

he can make sure he's kept in line," Sullivan went on without missing a beat.

Lizzie smiled and rubbed her belly with one hand. "Grand-children, Father," she said. "Plural."

Sullivan stared at her, coming closer to a smile than Zeke had ever seen him. "Grandchildren," he said, nodding in a greatly pleased manner.

Zeke watched him, thinking how the old man's legacy had changed so drastically from hatred to forgiveness. Perhaps what his father had said was true. Perhaps national pride was only part of a man's heritage. Only part of the legacy he would leave.

Perhaps his one most important strength would be to pass on to his own children the legacy his father would leave him. And yes, the legacy his grandfather would leave him, too.

The choice was his as much as it was either of theirs.

The End

MORE WESTERNS ARE in the works. I would appreciate a positive review on Amazon.